No Small Caper

A Tiny House Mystery, Book One

By Cynthia Hickey

Enjoy!
Cynthia Hickey

ISBN-13: 978-1-947523-42-5
ISBN-10: 1-947523-42-

DEDICATION

To all those who love a fun, rollicking good time in a clean who-dunnit..

Chapter One

"It's your job now to keep these crazies in line, Miss Turley." Lenora Rice of Heavenly Acres dropped a heavy key ring into my outstretched hand. Her gaze raked over me. "You don't look big enough for this job."

"Call me CJ." Excitement over my new position and beautiful home bubbled up like an Arkansas hot spring. I set down Caper, the spaniel-mix puppy I'd inherited and let her explore.

"I don't need to call you anything. I'm outta here. Good luck." The woman scrunched up her nose and turned away.

"Wait. Can't you give me some pointers? What do you mean by crazies?"

"Oh." She handed me a folder. "Here are the lists of renters and homeowners. Crazies? Like a bunch of twisted trees. You'll meet all kinds. It's up to you to monitor the grounds, see to repairs, collect rent and lot fees, etc. You're like…a leasing agent. Yeah, like that. Good chance you'll never see the owner. He's a recluse. Make friends with the man in house number seven. Name is Eric Drake. He's a park ranger and knows all there is to know about the area. There's food in the fridge—not a lot, just the essentials—until you make it to the store. No cars in the community. Everyone has other means of transportation from the parking lot to their home. It's a quiet place… most of the time."

I glanced at the concrete path that circled the lake. "That's it?"

"Yep. Might as well get settled and start meeting the kooks. Oh, and there's been a rash of robberies. Might want to look into that." She spun around, rushed to an older model sedan and sped away, leaving me standing with boxes piled around my feet. I heaved a sigh and regarded the green and white house the size of my parents' bedroom that sat on wheels.

The fifth key I tried unlocked the door to my new home. I stepped into a bright and airy room painted white with green trim to match the exterior. A forest-green love seat sat across from an entertainment center that housed a small television with room for my books, thank goodness. A counter ran along one wall with a single sink and a two-burner stove. Under the counter were nestled a washer/dryer combo, a tiny fridge, and cupboards. A small door led to a walk-in shower and compost toilet. Stairs with drawers inserted into each step led to a loft where a queen-size memory-foam mattress took up most of the space. I could just stand in the center of my "bedroom."

On each side of the bed were closets and

drawers that extended from floor to ceiling. My tiny home had everything I needed. With a happy sigh, I headed outside to drag in my boxes. Soon I realized how small my space was as I struggled to find a place for everything, but somehow I managed. A bookshelf and pretty storage boxes at the foot of my bed would help, so I made a note to purchase those as soon as possible. Until then, I piled the boxes on their sides and used them in place of a book case.

I grabbed a protein bar from the food items I'd thought to bring, shut Caper up in the house since I couldn't trust the little scamp not to get into trouble, and headed to a fairly new golf cart with bright red seats. The key hung in the ignition. Strange thing to do if robbers were milling around. Still, with a couple of hours of daylight left, I decided to drive through the community. I could meet those out and about, and the rest could wait until the next day. I clapped my hands, eager to get started, then headed down the path.

Trees lined my way with colorful homes appearing now and again. To my left, Lake Blue Waters, aptly named, sparkled in the late afternoon sun. Already peace started to erase the stress caused from taking care of a dying grandmother. I'd quit a job as a 911 operator to care for Gammy and when she died, I wanted something more...relaxing. When I'd spotted the ad in the paper for overseer of Heavenly Acres, I jumped at the opportunity.

"Hello." I stopped the cart in front of a home the color of bananas with purple gingerbread trim. An elderly woman wearing the largest floppy hat I'd ever seen straightened from her bed of peonies.

"I'm CJ Turley, the new overseer."

"I'm Mrs. Snyder, you can call me Mags." She pushed her hat off her face and narrowed her eyes. "How old are you?"

"Twenty-six. Why?" Strange question when you first meet someone.

"I can see you're going to need my help. Why they hired a child is beyond me. I'm sure you're aware we have a thief?"

"I've heard as much." I grinned. "I'm happy for all the help I can get. Has anyone called the police?"

"That handsome park ranger is responsible for this community, for the most part. Good thing, because the local police department, which has all of three officers, aren't worth squat. Come in and have a cup of tea." She turned without waiting for an answer and disappeared into her home.

Shrugging, I turned off the cart, pocketed the key, and followed her into a house so reminiscent of my grandmother's it brought tears to my eyes. Doilies and afghans covered every available surface. Family portraits filled the walls. She'd managed to cram so many treasures into the place it left little room to walk. A calico cat blinked up at me from the sofa. "Hello, gorgeous."

The cat hissed and darted to the loft only to appear on a ledge that circled the home. She peered down at me with big green eyes.

"Callie isn't friendly to strangers, but she won't bite." Mrs. Snyder fetched two mismatched tea cups, filled them, and handed one to me. "There's sugar and cream on the coffee table."

One sniff of the tea, mint green, and I knew I didn't need anything added. "Cute home."

"Too much stuff, but at my age, you don't want to get rid of anything. I've lost a set of emerald earrings to that robbing scoundrel, so I'm relying on you to find them." She slid sideways into a rocking chair across from me.

"What about the ranger?"

"Eric's working on it." She sipped her drink. "He's a busy man, so don't go bothering him."

Yes, ma'am. "Can you tell me about the other residents?"

"Houses one through seven are owners, the rest renters and I think only ten, eleven, and twelve are occupied right now. You're in number one, of course. There's a young married couple in two that stay to themselves. Newlyweds." She chuckled. "A middle-aged widower in three, a single harlot in four, a single mom in six, I'm in five, but you know that. It's suppertime, so don't go knocking on any doors. Wait until morning."

Bossy woman, but I could tell we would be great friends. "I'm just getting acquainted with the area tonight."

"Good. You have a head on your shoulders." She stood and removed the cup from my hand. "My shows are on. See you tomorrow. I'm here to help."

My eyes widened. "Of course."

She rushed me outside.

Laughing, I resumed my ride around the lake, pleased with how orderly and kept up the yards were. The "harlot" in four was the only house that needed improvement. Weeds grew up around the tires of her red and white house, a few shingles looked loose, nothing that couldn't be fixed. I'd approach the subject with her when I introduced myself.

Slowing down, I approached number seven, hoping to catch a glimpse of the handsome park ranger. The door opened, and he didn't disappoint. A man who had to stand over six feet in his socks with hair the color of milk chocolate and eyes the color of coffee stepped onto a postage-sized porch. He leaned on the wood railing.

"Good afternoon."

"Good afternoon." I stopped. "I'm CJ Turley, the new overseer."

"Eric Drake, ranger." A dimple winked in his cheek. "You're a lot prettier than Ms. Rice."

My face flushed, and I patted my almost black hair, pleased I'd let it hang loose around my shoulders. I'd spent so much time caring for Grams the last five years, good-looking men were foreign to me, unless they were over the age of sixty. "Uh, thanks."

"Where you headed?"

"Just getting familiar with the area."

He hopped off the porch, wearing flip-flops on his feet, and climbed into the cart. "Then I'm the best guide you'll get. Have you met anyone else?"

"Mrs. Snyder." My hands trembled as I steered back onto the path.

"Crusty, lovable soul." He placed his arm along the seat back. "I guess she told you about the other owners?"

I nodded, my mouth drying up as his fingers

brushed my shoulder. He moved, and I sighed, silly enough to hope he'd put them back. "Anything I need to know about my job?"

"Do you know how to fix things?"

I grinned. "I do. My father treated me like a son. I can even rebuild engines, with the proper tools."

"You sure don't look like a boy." He leaned over and peered at my face. "Grey eyes. I'd wondered."

There went the dreaded flush again. Experience had taught me that my face was as red as a berry. I cleared my throat. "You're a flirt."

"Guilty." He laughed, not seeming in the least bit embarrassed. "You're a welcome sight, CJ."

"I'm sure you see lots of sights in the forest."

"Animals, not pretty girls. Stop right here. You don't want to miss this."

I obeyed. "Oh." The setting sun kissed the lake with gold. Yes, I was going to like Heavenly Acres. Movement in the bushes to my right drew my attention.

A teenage boy jumped up, a red laptop under his arm, and darted away.

"Hey." I leaped from the cart and gave chase. A yapping behind me alerted me to the fact Caper had escaped the house, unless… "That's my laptop." Would we catch the thief on the first day?

"Hold back." Eric, now barefoot, bolted past me.

The boy dropped the laptop in a bush and dove into the lake. Eric splashed after him but gave up and trudged back dripping. "I guess we know who the thief is."

I retrieved my laptop and dog, putting both in the golf cart. "I'll have all the locks on the houses changed tomorrow." I stared after the swimming culprit. "Have you seen him before?"

"No, but my guess is he came from the campgrounds across from us. I'll ask around in the morning." He swept Caper into his arms and climbed back in the cart, keeping my pup in his lap. Lucky girl. "Cute dog."

"She's a rascal. I inherited her when Gammy died." I ruffled the dog's head. That boy could have caused her to be lost, and despite the trouble she caused more often than not, I enjoyed her company. I stared across the lake. Eric wouldn't be the only one asking questions the next day.

Chapter Two

Since I had the essentials in groceries, I decided to pay a visit to the Lake Blue Waters campground before heading into town. Caper perched on the golf cart seat next to me, her dark nose sniffing the air.

Few of the tiny house residents stirred at seven a.m., at least not outside. Lights shined in number four, five, and seven. Anxious to start my quest to catch a thief, I sped by without stopping. There would be plenty of hours in the day to introduce myself.

Fires burned in the campground. Folks seemed to be up and about earlier after sleeping in a tent. I nodded and smiled, keeping my eyes peeled for a teenage boy with sticky fingers.

Eric stepped into the path.

I hit the brake.

"What are you doing here, CJ?"

"Same as you, I reckon." I smiled.

He frowned. "This is my job; over there is

9

yours."

"No, it's my job to care for the residents *over there*. That's what I'm doing. Trying to stop the culprit that keeps taking their things." I leaned my arms on the steering wheel. "I doubt a teenage boy stealing for a joint is dangerous."

"You don't know why he's stealing. It could be for something other than drugs or for someone else." Eric crossed his arms. "Although that is a good reason for a teen to steal."

"Then hop on and we'll search together. Either way I'm going."

The corner of his mouth quirked. He grabbed the pole supporting the top and swung onto the seat, again scooping Caper into his lap. "You are a stubborn gal."

I grinned. "You have no idea. Where to?"

"Folks are used to me patrolling the sites, so follow the path." He ruffled my pup's fur and baby talked to her. *Be still my heart.*

Campers turned to look as we drove by, but not one of them was the boy we searched for. "This was a waste of time."

"The boy could be sleeping. He had to have run through here," Eric said. "We'll ask some questions. Stop the cart." Tucking Caper under his arm like a football, he approached a site of four women around my age.

Not wanting to be left behind, I scampered after him, taking the cart key with me. I stood to the side and a little behind to see how the women responded to a handsome ranger with a cute dog.

Oohs and aahs filled the air. Caper ate up the

attention, her fluffy tail wagging with the speed of a hummingbird's wings. While the women fawned over the dog, they shot doe-eyed looks at Eric.

"If we'd known you covered these campgrounds," a buxom brunette said, "we'd have come here sooner."

"I say we plan another girls' weekend right away," a blonde replied.

I rolled my eyes. Is this how women flirted now?

"I'm glad you're enjoying your stay." Eric grinned. "Mind if I ask you a few questions?"

"We weren't too loud, were we?" A plump woman with light brown hair paled. "We did have a lot of wine last night."

"No, ma'am. We're searching for a teenage boy wearing grey jeans and a blue and white striped shirt. He swam across the lake last night."

"I haven't seen anyone." An African American woman shook her head. "What if he drowned? Maybe he's lying on the shore somewhere."

I hadn't thought of that. Now that she mentioned it, we hadn't seen him climb from the water. "Eric?"

A muscle ticked in his jaw. "I'll get some people out here to search the water. Thank you, ladies." He headed back toward the cart.

I jogged after him. "Is it possible?"

"It's always possible." He sighed. "I hope that isn't the case. I'm the one that chased him into the water." He unclipped a radio from his belt and put in the call to send searchers and divers to the lake. When he'd finished, he climbed back into the cart.

"We keep asking questions. He may not have drowned. The boy belongs to someone. If he's missing, they'll cry an alarm."

Hope sprang anew. "We'll stop at each site."

He patted my hand. "I like your spirit."

That flush again. Ugh. I drove to the next occupied spot and followed Eric to a family of six where he repeated the same questions.

The father scowled. "Get Danny up. The rest of you kids stay out of the way and keep quiet."

A thin woman ducked into the tent, appearing a moment later with the very young man we sought. He took one look at us and darted away.

Eric shoved Caper into my arms and gave chase. "Oh no you don't." He tackled the boy to the ground before he could reach the water. "What's with you and swimming?"

"Blue ribbon swim team." The boy's face reddened.

Eric pulled the boy to his feet and marched him back to those of us waiting. "Sir, I need to ask your son some questions."

"He's my stepson. Ask his mom for permission." The man poked at a fire with a stick.

Shrugging, Eric turned to the frazzled woman. "How long have y'all been here?"

"A few weeks," she muttered. "We, uh, lost our house."

"Your son is stealing for money?"

"Maybe." She tucked a greasy strand of hair behind her ear, drawing notice to a pair of emerald earrings.

"Did he give you those?" I asked.

She quickly pulled her hair forward. "Yes, but he said he found them on the ground." She removed them from her ears and held them out to me. "I guess you know whom they really belong to."

"I do." I pocketed the jewelry. "Danny tried taking my laptop yesterday and let my dog out. She could have been lost." I hugged Caper until she started to squirm.

"I never told him to steal."

"Why don't you fill us in?" Eric pressed the boy into a camp chair.

"I wanted to help my family."

"How about getting a job?" Eric crossed his arms.

"I still have some of the things he took," his mother said. "I'll fetch them."

"Eric, can I talk to you?" I motioned my head for us to step a bit away from the family. "I want to help them."

"The boy will have to answer for his crimes, CJ."

"I know, but I can put them up in one of the rentals, he can work off what he's already sold, and his father can do maintenance and cleanup for the roof over their head."

"They'll still need money."

"We'll figure it out."

"What if you need their rental?"

"Again, we'll figure it out." I returned to the family. "I'm CJ Turley, overseer of the community across the lake. What are your names?"

The man glanced up. "I'm Roy Olson, my wife is named Tammy, you've met Danny. The girl is

Amanda and the littlest is Teddy. I reckon you're going to arrest the oldest?"

"I will have to take him in, yes." Eric narrowed his eyes at Danny. "I need a list of all the things you've taken."

"I've got a notebook in the tent." Tammy ducked in and emerged with a notebook and pencil. "Start writing." She shoved them in her son's hands.

When he'd finished, he handed the list to Eric who scanned the page. "This is only a few things. Where are the others?"

"That's all I took." The boy's shoulders slumped.

Eric exhaled heavily. "Looks like we still have a thief. Come on, son."

"Wait." I told the family of my offer.

Roy's brow furrowed. "I'm a good handyman. Tammy could maybe put up fliers to clean the houses or maybe get paid to clean up the campgrounds. We don't like charity, Miss, but I've run out of options. My kids need a roof over their heads, even a tiny one."

Tammy's face brightened. "There's lots of things I can do. I used to do people's shopping for them, you know? The ones too old or busy to shop for themselves. I've got references, and I'm bonded."

"Great. I'll be your first customer." I grinned. "Come by house number one later and I'll give you my list."

"Before you take Danny away," Roy said. "He needs to be the one to return the stolen items. Not you."

"I don't have a problem with that," Eric said. "Let's go. I'll bring him to house number thirteen later."

"Why thirteen?" I asked as we headed back to the community.

"It's one of the biggest. It'll still be crowded, but so is number six. That woman has five kids under the age of twelve."

We left a note at each house of the items stolen by Danny, passed by the ones whose thief was still at large, and then parked in front of Mags'. This ought to be interesting. I dug the earrings from my pocket and handed them to Danny. "Don't run or I'll chase you down in this cart and drive over your feet so you can't ever run again." Harsh, but effective.

The boy nodded, high spots of color on his cheeks, and jumped from the back of the cart where he'd held on during our drive back. He approached Mags, who straightened from her flower bed. "I brought your earrings back."

"You're the scoundrel who took them?" She looked him up and down. "You don't look like a thief."

"I'm not, usually." He scuffed at the dirt with a well-worn gym shoe.

"His family has fallen on hard times," Eric said. "I'm taking him in, but he'll be working around here, same as his family, once he's released."

Mags nodded. "Good. A boy needs to pay when he's done something wrong. That's how they learn." She tilted her head. "I've some honest work for you, if you've time after paying your dues."

"No, ma'am, I'll be working for her." He jerked his head toward me. "But my mother will be looking for paid work."

"Good. I've some old letters I want typed into a computer. My arthritic fingers don't like the task anymore. Send her my way when you're settled." Mags nodded toward me and returned to her gardening.

"That wasn't so bad. Hop back on, and I'll drive you to the parking lot," I said.

I stopped next to the Ford truck Eric said was his and watched as he drove away with a subdued Danny. Things could have been worse. A lot worse. The boy could have washed up on shore, and they would have had to tell his downtrodden family of his death. Instead, Eric had taken back the call to sweep the lake and all would be fine.

"One more stop, then time for lunch." I patted Caper's head and sped toward house thirteen to wait for the Olson family

I didn't wait long. They pulled up in a beat-up Van Caravan. I handed Roy the key. "It'll be tight, but it doesn't leak. After you come by my place in the morning, Tammy, there's a job for you at number five. Roy, check in with me first thing each morning for a list of jobs starting tomorrow."

"Much obliged, Miss Turley. You won't regret this, and I'll keep Danny in line."

"Call me CJ." I smiled and waved as I headed home. It had been a good day. One thief caught and a family helped.

Again, I'd made the right decision in taking the overseer job. Tomorrow, I'd search for thief number two.

Chapter Three

A knock at the door had me scurrying from bed and down the stairs. I yanked open the door to the sound of Caper's yapping, and greeted Roy and Tammy. "Sorry. I overslept. Come on in." Thank goodness I slept in shorts and a tee-shirt. I grabbed two sheets of notebook paper from the counter.

"Roy, I'd like the lawn cared for at number four. If the woman who lives there complains, send her my way. Tell her this is the one and only time we will clean her yard for her. That responsibility is hers." I removed a key from the ring hanging on a hook on my wall. "This will open the garden shed. There's an extra golf cart in there, key in the ignition. The rest of the list should be self-explanatory, but if not, come see me. Tammy, here is my shopping list and my cell phone number." I handed her a hundred dollars in twenties. "Call me if you can't find what I need." I smiled. "Any questions?"

With shell-shocked eyes, they both shook their

heads. I tended to be a bit...zealous at times. Hopefully, they'd grow used to me. I rubbed my hands together and poured the coffee that had percolated overnight, then stepped outside onto my tiny porch and contemplated what I'd do first that day.

There were still a thief to catch and residents to meet. Since it was Saturday, I figured most of the community would be home.

Eric drove by in a military-green golf cart and waved on his way around the lake. I smiled and waved back. Go investigate, handsome man. I'd be doing my own later on. I went back inside and changed into a tank top and denim capris.

A few minutes later, with Caper on the seat next to me, we headed off to meet the people I'd be serving. All the homes were white with different colored trim. House number two sported a lovely shade of sky blue.

A bi-racial couple glanced up from a bistro-style table in front of their house and smiled. "Good morning." I climbed from the cart. "I'm CJ Turley, the new overseer."

"I'm Mark Boyles," a young man with sandy-colored hair and gold-rimmed glasses offered his hand. "This is my new bride, Linda."

"Nice to meet both of you." I shook his hand and looked into a flawless face. Skin the color of creamed coffee, jet-black curls, and milk-chocolate eyes. "What do you do for a living?"

"We're both teachers," Linda said. "Elementary. We love it here, and I'm so glad it's summer break so we can enjoy the lake."

"I think I will enjoy living here too and hope we'll be great friends. Is there anything I can do for you? We have a handyman now."

"The drain in the bathroom clogs up," Mark said. "I've been pouring clog remover down it, but it doesn't last."

"Got it. I'll send him around today or tomorrow. We also have a gal that will do shopping or other jobs for a reasonable price." I climbed in the cart and headed to number three. I hadn't said I hoped Linda and I would be friends just to be nice. I could use a girlfriend. Taking care of Gammy had left me with a non-existent social life. Maybe I could host a community barbeque to fix the problem.

The door to number three opened when I turned off the golf cart and a silver-haired fox opened the door. Dentist-whitened teeth flashed. "Hello."

"Good morning." I approached him, hand extended and introduced myself.

"Dave Lincoln. It's nice to meet you, although I wouldn't think a pretty little thing like you would want to hide away out here."

Hmm. I tilted my head. "Is that what you're doing? Hiding?"

He laughed. "No, just living the simple life. I retired early, and nothing sounded better than a house on the lake."

"What did you do?"

"Imports and exports, that type of thing." He shrugged. "Boring really."

In the movies, that usually meant a nefarious means of making a living. "Have you been a victim of the thief?"

"No, I've installed an alarm system on my tiny house." He grinned as if he'd done something remarkable, and stuck out his chest.

"Is there anything that needs repairing in your house?"

"No, but if you're the one doing the fixing, I'll make sure something breaks."

Eew. "Nope. That would be up to our new handyman. Have a good day." I needed a shower. Caper must not have liked him either because she stayed in her seat, her eyes never leaving me, during my conversation with the man.

The nice summer morning had folks outside it seemed. The "harlot," a pretty woman in her thirties with dyed blond hair, which I was pretty sure had the help of extensions to fall all the way to her waist, sat on her porch with a cup of coffee. I smiled at the bright red trim around her house. "Good morning. I'm CJ Turley."

"Amber Jones." Her teeth flashed under scarlet lipstick. "Come on up and sit."

I scooped Caper into my arms and accepted her invitation. "I'm making the rounds and introducing myself."

"So, you've met Mags, I assume."

I nodded and waited for her next sentence.

"She doesn't like me much." She chuckled. "You'd think a woman would be nicer to her granddaughter."

"What?" Really?"

She nodded. "Says I wear too much artificial help to look pretty. Maybe I do, but I like the way I look."

"Calling you a har—" I bit my lip.

"Seems a bit harsh?" She shrugged. "I'm divorced, childless, and like men. She's entitled to her opinion, the crusty old bat. Add in the fact that I'm a nurse and former flight attendant, who are all people of low moral fiber, you know." She sighed. "I love that old woman, but she drives me crazy. I live here in order to keep an eye on her, but do not tell her I said that. She's very independent."

"I got that impression." I stood, liking the woman very much for watching over someone despite the fact the someone didn't seem to like her. "I think you and I will get along just fine."

"I think we will too." Amber smiled. "Have a great day."

Mags wasn't outside, but she was pacing past her windows. Since I'd already met her, I continued to number six where five children ran around the postage stamp-sized yard. A black Labrador barked and chased them, sending Caper into another yapping session, creating unbelievable racket.

Lucy Flower, a frazzled woman maybe a year or two under thirty stepped out of the house and yelled for everyone to hush up or she'd beat their butts so hard their noses would bleed. She froze and forced a smile when she noticed me. "Sorry. I don't really beat my children. If I did, they might be better behaved."

I commanded Caper to stay and approached the house, again introducing myself. "I'm coming around to see if there is anything I can do?"

"How about giving me a break?" She wiggled her eyebrows.

"I know someone who might be willing for a reasonable price." I wasn't sure whether Tammy would be desperate enough to watch this brood for any amount of money, but one never knew. "I'll send her by."

"Let me introduce you to my brood, the terrors of the community. Rose is the oldest at almost thirteen, then you have Daisy, she's eleven, Briar is nine, Lilly is seven, and little Sage is five. Since my parents gave me a boring name, I named my kids after plants. Their no-good father had to go and die on me, leaving me with a small life insurance policy and a mound of debt, hence the reason we're crammed in this tiny house." She smiled to take some of the sting from her words. "No, the only thing my husband did wrong was die. He was a wonderful man, but I'm a little angry anyway."

I understood. When Gammy died, and my parents before her, I felt abandoned. I smiled at the dark-haired, dark-eyed children who now clustered around us like a bouquet. "They're adorable."

"I think so."

After making sure she didn't have any repairs that needed doing, I finished my rounds of the houses and headed for the campground. I did a cursory drive through, saw nothing out of the ordinary, and parked near the restrooms to wait for someone who looked like they could talk the hind leg off a mule. Those were the type of people who gave you information they didn't know they had, according to Gammy anyway.

I let Caper out to run around and waited. As I was about to give up, a woman in a bright pink sweat suit approached the building, pulling a wagon of cleaning supplies behind her. Perfect. "Hello."

"Howdy." The woman's bright blue gaze focused on me. She dressed much older than she looked, although it was hard to see what she looked like with a floppy hat tied low over her face with a floral scarf. "You waiting for someone?"

"You." I grinned. "I'm on a scouting mission, and you are just the person to answer my questions."

"Not interested in anything you're selling." She put a hand on the women's bathroom door.

"I'm not selling anything." I hopped from the cart and followed. "There's been a rash of robberies in Heavenly Acres. Have you noticed the same over here?"

She whirled. "Do I look like a thief?"

I took a step back. "No, ma'am, but you do look like nothing gets past you."

"You are correct." She stepped into a stall and slammed the door. "I have work to do. Go away."

"You aren't one of the campers?"

"No, I live in the trailer at the entrance. It's up to me to collect the fees and run off the riff-raff. If I can't, then Mr. Drake does."

I leaned against the brick wall. "He's helping me look for the thief. I hoped you'd help."

"How does it feel to be disappointed?" The sound of a brush on porcelain reached my ears.

"What's your name?"

She shoved open the door. "Are you hard of hearing?"

"No, but I don't understand your animosity

toward me."

She exhaled heavily. "I don't know about any robberies in the campgrounds. If they're happening, no one is telling me. That means the problem is most likely with one of your own." She moved to the next stall.

Maybe my instincts about the type of people who were talkative weren't as good as my grandmother's. I stepped outside and located Caper sniffing around the dumpsters. "Come on, girl. This was a waste of time."

Back in the cart, I drove to the one and only trailer on the lake. Old, but clean, with a bit of rust. Out front a vinyl canopy shaded a plastic table and two chairs. Ms. Grouchy Pants most likely lived alone considering only one pair of rain boots sat outside the door. I wasn't used to people not liking me and had to admit it stung a bit.

Wait a minute. Sweat suit? It had to be approaching eighty degrees. None of my business. I headed home. I'd ask Eric later what the woman's name was. I bet she treated him a lot nicer then she had me.

Speaking of the handsome devil. Eric sat outside my house and grinned when I pulled up.

"Making the rounds, I see." He propped a foot on the runner of the cart.

"Here and across the lake. Met a nasty-tempered woman."

His brow furrowed. "Who? Everyone seems nice to me."

"The woman who lives in the trailer and cleans the bathrooms."

He scratched his head. "A man lives there. Mr. Robinson. Unless he got himself a girlfriend recently, he's a confirmed bachelor."

"Then who was the woman cleaning the restroom?"

Eric hopped into the cart. "Let's go see if we can catch her."

Chapter Four

We sped around the campground and saw no sign of Ms. Pink Sweat Suit. I parked in front of the trailer where a man so thin a stiff wind might blow him over greeted us. Mr. Robinson, I presumed.

"Howdy, Ranger," he said, grinning. "Who's the pretty gal?"

"Good morning, Robinson. This is the new overseer at Heavenly Acres, CJ Turley." Eric hopped from the cart. "We're looking for a woman in a pink sweat suit claiming to be the camp overseer. You haven't gotten yourself hitched, have you?"

"Heaven forbid." Robinson shuddered. "I haven't seen a woman like that around."

"I met her at the bathrooms," I said. "She was cleaning."

"Heck, then, let's keep her around. I could use the help. Come and sit a spell." He plopped down at a wooden picnic table. "Tell me why she's so important."

Eric and I joined him. "We're looking for someone stealing from the tiny house community," I said. "When I saw her with a wagon of cleaning supplies, I thought she might have some answers. Those in housecleaning usually know everything that happens."

He rubbed his chin. "So that's where my wagon and stuff went. Haven't found anything else missing though. She's obviously crazy or using the supplies as a cover."

Both in my opinion. "She kept her head down, so I didn't get a good look at her face."

"Guilty." He slapped the table, cackling.

"Don't go passing judgment yet," Eric said. "She could be one of the hundred eccentrics roaming this area. We'll keep looking."

"I'll keep my eyes open for the thief." Robinson stood. "Don't be a stranger, Ranger and CJ. Come by for coffee sometime. I don't aim to ever settle down, but the occasional visit from friends is welcome."

Gammy would have said that a man so opposed to getting married would find himself hopelessly in love before he could say, "No way." Maybe I'd do a little matchmaking if I found the right woman.

"It was good to meet you." I smiled and climbed back into the cart. "I'll take you up on that coffee someday." I turned to Eric. "Where to?"

"I've got to take a hike, literally. Once or twice a month, I patrol the trails. Want to come?"

"No, I've got to get back and check on the Olson family. My supplies should be in by now.

Rain check?"

"Sure thing."

I dropped him off near his own cart, then hurried home. Sure enough bags waited on my porch. Stuffed down inside one was an envelope with my change. I'd have to let Tammy know to keep it until she could hand it over to me. I didn't need any of my things going missing.

After letting Caper out to do her business, I carried my things into the house and put together the cubed setup I planned on using for books and baskets to hold some of the things that wouldn't fit in the miniscule closet. I set the cubby at the edge of the loft to serve as a wall to keep me from falling over when I was half asleep. A few nails through the bottom secured it in place. Voilà.

I took Caper with me on my way to see the Olsons, stopping in front of Mags' house when I spotted her yelling at Danny and waving her finger in his face.

"What's wrong?" I called from my seat.

"A necklace and a tennis bracelet went missing right after this boy pulled weeds for me." Mags crossed her arms.

"I swear I never went into the house." Danny copied her stance. "No one can walk in there anyway. You have too much junk."

"Aha. You have been inside."

"No, I could see enough through the open door."

"I don't leave my door open when I go for my morning walk."

He shrugged. "It was open when I came back from the bathroom."

"My bathroom?"

"No, ma'am. I told you I didn't go inside." He rolled his eyes. "Are you hard of hearing?"

This was going nowhere. I hopped down and stepped between them. "Did you lock your door, Mags?"

She lifted her chin. "I can't remember."

It looked to me like she'd been hit by the other thief. "May I go inside and look around?" I'd seen enough cop shows to notice anything out of the ordinary.

"Sure. I'll stay out here and watch this scoundrel."

Leaving Caper outside, I entered Mags' house, stopping inside the door. "Where was the necklace?"

"Bedroom."

Her house was a bit larger than mine with not only a loft, but a small bedroom off the living area. Dirty footprints led in that direction from the front door. I'd have to compare the tread with that of Mags' and Danny's shoes.

I walked around the prints, not wanting to mess them up in case we did call the police, and entered a bedroom so bright and white it hurt my eyes. On a small table next to the bed rested an open jewelry box. Other than the muddy footprints, nothing seemed out of the ordinary or out of place, although it was hard to tell with all the clutter. Mags' cat peered at me from under the white dust ruffle on the bed.

I stepped back outside. "Let me see the bottom of both of y'all's shoes." Puzzled expressions on their faces, they both lifted up a foot. I smiled. "The thief left behind a clue." I snapped a photo with my cell phone, then sent Eric a text, and called the local cops.

A squad car pulled up within fifteen minutes with two officers. Their badges showed Officer Milton and Perk.

"What's the problem?" Officer Milton, a man who looked as if he enjoyed his doughnuts too much, whipped open a small notebook. "You've been robbed?"

"Yes." Mags sniffed. "A gold chain right out of my jewelry box."

He took down our names and reason for being at Mags' house. "Any idea who?" He narrowed his eyes at Danny. "You again."

"It wasn't him," I said. "There are muddy footprints inside that don't match any of ours."

"You went inside?" His brows rose.

"I didn't touch anything."

He motioned his head for Officer Perk to enter the house. "Where's Drake?"

"On patrol," I said. "As the overseer, I felt it my job to handle things."

"By not informing us we still had a thief?"

"I'm letting you know now." I sighed. "I just started here, and there's been a lot to adjust to. Can we move forward with this and help each other?"

"You'll stay out of it." He marched past us and into the house.

"I told you the cops here aren't worth much," Mags said. "They were called once before and did little to nothing. It wasn't them who caught Danny, and I bet it won't be them who catch this thief."

I had to agree with her. "We still have to let them try."

"And sit on our rear ends doing nothing?" Her eyes widened. "No, ma'am, you get your skinny little self busy solving this while I still have jewelry left. And I'll help you."

"Me too." Danny gave a definitive nod. "I'm all over this community doing this and that. I'm observant."

"Don't forget you also know how a thief thinks," Mags said.

"Sure." I grinned. What could possibly go wrong with the three of us working together?

After dropping Danny off, I thanked Tammy for doing my shopping. I made mention that she might want to let Mags settle down a bit before heading her way to type.

"If you have time," Roy said, "I found something during my wanderings I thought you might want to see."

"Sure. Hop in."

Seconds later, we followed the path to the edge of the lake between the community and the campground. "Stop here," he said. "We have to walk the rest of the way."

How in the world had he found something off the beaten path during a normal work day? With Caper tucked securely under one arm, I followed Roy down an overgrown path. He pushed a low-hanging branch out of the way and stepped back for me to proceed ahead of him.

Oh. A cathedral, similar to one I'd seen in

Eureka Springs, but half the size, sat in gross disrepair. Most of the glass in the windows that made up the walls had been shattered, although some were still intact. "A church."

"That ain't the best part. Come on." He led me further down the path to where a large cross rose above its surroundings. "I found some old electrical wiring. I think this lit up at one time."

Exhaling slowly, I marveled in the quiet beauty of the place. I ran my hand over the white of the cross. "Can it be repaired?"

"Sure, it can. The cross will be easier than the church. That will be costly."

"I'll come up with the money somehow." This place needed to be restored. I shoved aside some ivy and entered the church.

A sleeping bag and propane lantern sat behind the leaning podium. Further searching revealed a propane stove and a box of foodstuff. I believed we'd found where our thief resided. Reluctantly, I called Officer Milton and told him where to find us.

It took some time, but he eventually arrived alone eating a burger. My stomach growled. He glanced around the church. "Bet this was nice once."

"Here are the things I mentioned." I led him behind the podium.

He glanced around. "Doesn't mean it's our thief. We have our share of homeless people."

"It could be though." Was the man stupid or lazy?

"Well, keep an eye out. Let us know if the person returns."

Seriously? "You want us to camp out here and wait for them? Don't you have an officer to do that? Remember, you told me to stay out of this investigation."

He narrowed his eyes. "I meant it too. Do not confront. Just pass on the info." He turned and strolled down the path, wadding up his burger wrapper.

Question answered. Catching the thief would be up to me. Obviously, Milton didn't want to be bothered.

"I have a game camera we can set up," Roy said, shrugging. "It won't let you catch the person, but might get a good enough shot of them that you can make an identification."

"Thank you, Roy." I needed to find Eric. He might have an idea.

"Absolutely not," he said, taking a bite out of a ham and cheese sandwich. I'd located him perched on a picnic table in the campground.

I eyed his food. If I didn't eat soon, I'd be hangry and fit to be tied. "Why not? The police are incompetent."

"This person might be dangerous. I'll do it." He smiled and handed me half the sandwich. "Eat it before you snatch it from my hands."

"I'm starving." I closed my eyes and took a bite. Mustard. Well, a starving woman couldn't be picky. "You can't be everywhere, Eric. I can help."

"It isn't your job."

"You aren't my boss."

"Very mature." He hopped from the table. "I'll keep you informed."

I scowled. "Maybe I'll be the one keeping you informed."

"Go home and eat, CJ. You're being unreasonable." He climbed into his golf cart. "I'll catch up with you later."

I planted my hands on my hips. The man could order me around all he wanted, but I'd still do what I wanted. Darn it. I wanted to tell him about my plans to renovate the church, but I couldn't say more than we found evidence that someone was living in it.

It didn't matter. I drove to the Olson house. Roy and I would set up a camera and catch the culprit ourselves.

Chapter Five

"That's the woman in the pink sweat suit."
I pointed at my laptop screen as Roy, Eric, and I
searched through the game cam pictures. The scent
of Eric's woodsy cologne made it hard to
concentrate. "I told you."

The woman shoved her meager belongings into
the wagon, along with the cleaning supplies, then
dragged it all out of the dilapidated building. She
glanced to her left, then to her right, and headed into
the brush.

"Yes, you did." Eric chuckled and straightened.
"She's packed up and gone now."

"She'll be back." I faced him. "She'll find a new
place to hide while she steals."

"Where is she putting the stolen items?" Roy
removed the Sim card from the laptop. "Because
they sure weren't in the church."

"Speaking of...I'd like to renovate the building.
Where can we purchase supplies for a reasonable
price?" The budget for the upkeep of the

community wouldn't stretch far enough.

"That cross is bright enough to land an airplane," Eric said. "It was unplugged years ago because the residents here complained."

"Too bad. I bet it's beautiful." I grinned.

"Let's see what you think when it sears your eyeballs. But, if you're serious, I'll see who we can find to replace the glass." Eric plopped a cap on his head. "I'm off to start the day. Try and stay out of trouble." He winked and exited my house.

That was my cue. I had renters moving into houses ten, eleven, and twelve that morning and wanted to give each place a quick once-over before they arrived. I clapped Roy on the shoulder. "Keep your eyes out for that woman."

"You bet." He flopped a tattered hat onto his head and proceeded out of the house in front of me.

After slipping my feet into a pair of fluorescent pink Crocs, I climbed into my golf cart, Caper at my side, and headed for the rentals. The three rented houses were identical to mine, including the green trim. A quick look through number ten showed everything was fine. I sat on the stoop to wait for the tenant to arrive. I'd scheduled them all half an hour apart in order to greet each one.

My mind focused on the woman in pink. For the life of me, I couldn't place her as one of the community's own, which meant she came from somewhere else. Town? Campground? Why live in an abandoned, falling-down building? I had no answers, but was determined to find some.

I plastered a smile on my face as a light blue Prius parked in front of me. "Behave, Caper." The pup sat and glanced up at me.

The woman climbing from the car stared in disdain at my dog. "I hope it doesn't have full reign. I don't like dogs in my house."

I bit my tongue and held out my hand. "Marcy Wilson? I'm CJ Turley, the overseer. Welcome to Heavenly Acres."

"It is a pretty place." She glanced at the lake. "Is swimming allowed?"

"Yes, and there are kayaks, canoes, and paddleboats available. I'm sure you'll enjoy your time here." I held out a clipboard for her to sign the lease, then gave her the keys.

She flipped a ponytail the color of cola over her shoulder. "Time will tell. Is it possible to get help unloading my things when the truck arrives?"

I nodded. "I'll hunt someone down and send them your way." I scooped up Caper, who had been unnaturally well-behaved, and climbed back into the golf cart to find Roy.

"I didn't realize unloading trucks was part of the job," he scowled.

"Just this once." I smiled. "You're actually here to do, well, whatever needs doing."

"Fine." He sped off in the direction of house number ten, muttering beforehand that she'd better give him a tip for helping.

Poor thing, living practically free in one of the houses. Doing whatever came up was his job. I spotted a dark blue sedan in front of house eleven. The tenant had arrived early.

A short wiry man pulled a box from his trunk, glancing up as I stopped. "You the boss?"

I chuckled. "CJ Turley at your service." I grabbed my clipboard and slid from the cart. "You look eager to move in."

"I am." He grinned. "Bob Guide. I've always wanted to live on a lake. After my divorce, I figured this was the perfect time."

"If you'll sign here, I'll hand over the keys and let you get busy." I told him to let me know if he needed anything, that we had a handyman ready to help, and that the park ranger worked at keeping the place safe. I felt it wise to leave out the thief on the loose.

We finished our business and I headed to number twelve. While Mr. Guide had been early, Mr. Jones arrived almost an hour late. I'd just climbed into the cart to leave when a battered Ford truck blocked my path.

"Sorry." A tall man pulled off a cowboy hat to reveal orange hair and approached me. "Got a flat." He whistled for a beagle to hop from the front seat. "This is Barney. Say hello to the fancy pup, boy."

Caper stuck her pert little nose in the air, clearly unimpressed when the other dog lifted its leg on the wheel of the house. I shared her sentiment, hoping the pet was housebroken. I stared at the mound of boxes in the back of the man's truck and couldn't help but wonder where he'd put it all.

"Sign here." I held out the clipboard. "I hope you'll enjoy it."

"Can't beat the view." He gave me a lecherous grin.

Eew. I hoped the man wouldn't be a problem. I forced a return smile and hightailed it out of there, not stopping until I reached my house where Mags sat on the steps.

"It's about time." She pushed to her feet. "How do you expect to catch a thief if you're always gone?"

"Doing my job?" I hopped from the cart. "What's up?"

"Roy told me you had pictures of the strange woman. I want to see them."

"Come on in." I led her into the house and opened the laptop on the fold-down table.

Mags glanced around the room. "You don't have much, do you?"

"I like things simple." Especially in small spaces. "Here she is."

Mags, smelling strongly of onion and garlic, leaned over the screen. "She walks like a man."

"What?" I peered at the video. "She didn't walk like a man when I spoke to her."

"Well, she does here."

Could we have more than one thief wearing pink? "I need to find Eric."

"He's probably over at that old man's trailer who runs the campground." Mags didn't sound impressed.

"I'll look there first. Thanks." I rushed back to the cart and sped around the lake.

Eric wasn't there. Mr. Robinson said I'd missed him by five minutes and that he had no idea where he went. Looking for him would be like looking for the proverbial needle in a haystack. We needed radios. What if I had an emergency?

I made another circle around the lake, slower

this time, and searched the people for a glimpse of someone in pink. Not a single soul fit the description. If the thief changed outfits, I'd never spot her, or him. Some of my enthusiasm for solving this mystery dimmed.

We had no money in the budget for security cameras, although they were needed. Maybe an email to the owner would result in some funds not only for security but for the church. It didn't hurt to ask.

I drove home and sent the email, praying the thefts wouldn't look unfavorably on my first few days on the job. I'd never met the owner of the property, just corresponded through emails. I got the impression the man or woman was eccentric and looked more on the community as a hobby of sorts. Something to do with their abundance of money. Just as in the past, the answer to my email returned within minutes.

"Yes." They'd send over a company this afternoon to install cameras. Guess it paid to have money. As for the church, they wanted an estimate first. Okay, I could get them that.

After a quick lunch of microwave noodles in broth, I met the security installers at the front gate. After introducing myself, I let them know I'd like cameras at the front and back entrance and in other locations that would cover every house, owned or rented.

"It'll take a few days to finish a job this big," the man said.

"That's fine." I clapped my hands together. This job was a cinch for me.

"What's going on?" Eric asked, stopping his cart next to me.

"Security cameras." I beamed. "I was looking for you. Do you have a minute?"

"For you? Always." That dimple winked in his cheek.

My face flushed and I moved closer to him, lowering my voice. I told him what Mags had said upon seeing the video. "Could she be right?"

"Possibly. It's something to consider. The cameras are a great idea. I'd suggested such to the previous overseer, but she couldn't be bothered."

"This gives me a chance to prove my worth. Nothing like a challenge right off to show a person what they're made of."

He laughed. "That's one way of looking at it."

"What in tarnation?" Mags marched to my side and crossed her arms. "This looks like an invasion of privacy."

"There won't be any cameras inside the houses," I said. "The community needs them."

"You ought to call a meeting before making such big changes."

"Settle down," Eric told her. "You know you've wanted this for months. You're just upset because it wasn't your idea this time."

The corner of her mouth twitched. "This will make catching the thief harder. They'll see the cameras."

"They're discreet." I pointed. "See? They look like leaves on the trees."

"Hmph. What about in the fall when the leaves fall off?"

I sighed. "You're being difficult."

"No, practical."

I approached the men installing the cameras and asked if they had something that would blend in with the tree better. They told me they had some the color of bark and would use those. I doubted it would make Mags any happier that I'd chosen to have them installed, but she'd have to get over it.

After returning to her and Eric, I said, "I'd like to schedule a community barbeque. How did Mrs. Rice communicate to everyone at once?"

"The bulletin board at the entrance, mostly," Mags said. "I still say you should call a meeting."

"Why? I've introduced myself to everyone already."

"Seems more professional. You're like…a small town mayor."

I couldn't hold back a laugh. "You're a riot, Mags. Oh, and Eric, you and I need radios. What if something happens and I can't find you?"

He nodded. "I'll bring one by you tonight." He leaned close and whispered, "a flier on the community board will suffice. I'll bring supper along with the radio."

I watched him drive away as my heart turned flips in anticipation of seeing him after work hours.

Chapter Six

I printed off the flier as Eric stepped through my open front door. "I smell pizza."

"Yep. I made a deep dish." He held out the pan so I could get a good look.

My eyes widened. "You made this?" I sniffed, savoring the aromas of sauce and cheese. "I'm impressed."

"I love cooking. My small house—not as tiny as what most people live in—has a great kitchen. My one must-have in a house." He set the pizza on the counter. "Paper plates?"

"Nope." I reached around him and grabbed two red ones from the plate holder on the wall. "No room for anything but the necessities." I smiled. While he cut and served our supper, I moved my laptop to a shelf, leaving the flier for him to go over.

"Cute." He set the plates down, then sat in one of my two folding chairs. "Definitely eye-catching."

I thought so. The bright blue letters on a yellow

background popped. I'd even added balloons along the sides. "It's a bit like the invitation to a child's birthday party, but I doubt it'll be missed among the other notices on the board."

He glanced around my home. "Where are the techs going to put the monitor for the cameras?"

"Software on my laptop." I cut the thick pizza into bite-sized pieces and popped one in my mouth. Hot, but heavenly. "I can take it with me wherever I go. A beep will sound when one of the cameras is activated after hours." I tapped my forefinger against my temple. "Always thinking."

"You're doing a great job here, CJ. The cameras were a wonderful idea. This way you can keep an eye on things without putting yourself in danger. Catching a thief isn't your job. Now you can stay here and do what you were hired to do." He smiled as if he'd said the most wonderful thing.

I leaned back and crossed my arms. "It *is* my job to keep the community safe."

"By calling the authorities when necessary." A wary look crossed his eyes.

"You sure have a lot of opinions regarding what I should or should not do."

"I'm trying to keep you from being hurt."

"That isn't your job." I stabbed my fork into another bite of pizza.

He put his hand over mine. "Let's not argue."

Then mind your own business. "I agree. The pizza is delicious. Let's talk about the barbeque. Where can I get the best pulled pork and ribs?"

"Me." He grinned and straightened. "I've got my grandfather's sauce recipe and love to barbecue.

I'll borrow a big grill from a friend of mine."

"Great. I'll send Tammy after the food the morning of." My tiny refrigerator barely held my own food much less enough for everyone.

"Sounds like a plan."

After we'd eaten our fill, Eric invited me to ride along with him as he patrolled the grounds before heading home. Not wanting to skip a chance to find the woman in pink or spend time with him, I agreed and wisely let him think I simply wanted his company. Not a lie at all. I did enjoy his company. If only he'd drop the high-handed, chauvinist views of letting a man handle the dangerous things. I had no intention of tackling the thief by any means, but I did want to find the scoundrel. Then, I could turn him over to the authorities. Maybe I needed a Taser so they wouldn't get away when I did find them.

"I can see the wheels turning in your head," Eric said as we drove toward the campground. "You threw every caution I said out the window, didn't you?"

"Of course not."

"Liar." His lips quirked. "Fine. Have it your way. It gives me more opportunity to keep my eyes on you. My eyes are happy when they're watching you."

And cue the flush, which increased when he reached over and held my hand. Not having many boyfriends growing up, and *nada* while caring for Grammy, I had no idea how to react to his attention. So I sat there with my lips clenched.

Eric chuckled, gave my hand a squeeze, then released me. "Your shyness is cute." He parked the cart on a small hill overlooking the lake.

The moon cast a silver path across a surface of glass—truly one of God's greatest works. "It's so beautiful here."

"One of my favorite places to sit and think." He slid from the cart and helped me out. "The flat rock over here makes the perfect place to sit." He led me to the boulder on the lake's bank.

Our shoulders touched. I couldn't remember a more perfect evening.

"If we're going to be finding this thief together, we need a plan," Eric said.

I smiled. "Mags and Danny are helping too."

He groaned. "Mags is about as subtle as a banshee screaming from the top of a tree."

"Yes, but not much gets past her."

"That is true. So, Miss Always Thinking, what's the plan?"

"I haven't gotten past the security cameras. I figured we'd wait and see if we pick up anything on those."

"So nothing for a few days."

I peered through the night at him. "You don't have to sound so relieved."

He laughed. "Nothing more has gone missing. Maybe the thief has moved on."

"Then I will have finished this particular job in record time." I bumped him with my shoulder.

As if taking the gesture as an invitation, his arm snaked around me and pulled me close. I didn't complain. The warmth of his chiseled body sent my nerves into overdrive, making the sounds of the night come alive with a serenade.

Wait. The snap of a twig wasn't part of the song. "Shh."

"I hear it," he whispered. He slowly stood and held out his hand when the sound came again. "Someone is out there."

My heart skipped a beat, but not in the "he's holding my hand again" kind of way. I pressed my lips together and let Eric lead me into the bushes.

As we moved, I began to think we hadn't been watched after all. Whoever was in front of us didn't seem to care if they were heard or not. While it might be strange to hike the woods at nine o'clock at night, it wasn't unheard of.

"There." Eric pointed. "Do you know him?"

I recognized the cowboy hat. "That's Red Jones, the renter in number twelve."

The man set a flashlight next to the lake and, using a small hand net, scooped something from the water. He plucked it from the net and dropped it into a bucket.

"He's fishing for crawdads." Eric shook his head, then grinned, his teeth flashing in the light of the moon. "That was fun."

"And didn't end in catastrophe." I returned his smile.

"Who's there?" Red whirled, pulling a gun from his waistband.

"That is a problem." Eric's expression etched like carved stone. "It's Eric Drake, park ranger, and CJ Turley, the overseer."

Red dropped his bucket and sprinted in the opposite direction.

"Aren't we going after him?" My eyes widened.

"I'm not chasing a man with a gun through the dark woods. I'll hunt him down tomorrow and see if he has a permit for that weapon. Come on. Let's get you home before we do run into something."

The next morning I woke to the sound of men's voices. The security people had arrived early. Eager to start the day but still enjoying the pleasure of the night before, I climbed out of bed, and grabbed a slice of leftover pizza for breakfast. I ate it cold while sipping my coffee and watched the workers from the window over my sink.

Mags was right. Making the cameras the color of the tree branches made them virtually invisible. If you didn't know they were there, you wouldn't see them. The only problem I could foresee—if the thief was one of the residents, he'd know the cameras were being installed. I shrugged. It might deter further crime regardless.

Once I woke up enough to face the day, I headed to the Olsons' to give Tammy a shopping list for the barbeque on Saturday. I liked having someone do my shopping. It made me feel important.

As I pulled up in front of their house, Roy came around the corner, the bucket and net belonging to Red in his hands. "Someone left these by the lake."

"I know who they belong to. Set them in the back, and I'll drop them off." I handed Tammy my list. "For Saturday morning."

She glanced over the sheet. "This is a lot of stuff."

"Yes, but don't worry. I've budgeted for such things." Hiring a handyman for the cost of a rental left repair funds in the black to be used for other things. "You don't need to worry about the money, Tammy. That's my job." I waved and headed for number twelve, not surprised to see Eric already there.

"Roy found the things you left behind." I slid from the cart and retrieved them from the back. "Returning lost items is not part of his job description."

"Sorry about that. Y'all startled me." Dave pushed his hat away from his eyes.

"Why'd you run?" I narrowed my eyes.

"Down girl," Eric said, his eyes twinkling. "He has a permit to carry."

"I don't like it. If he had a trigger finger, he'd have shot us. What if one of the children had been playing in the woods?"

"I'll be more careful," Red promised. "It's a side effect of my war days."

"Thank you for your service," I said automatically, not appeased by the fact he was a veteran. He'd still drawn his gun on us. I set the bucket and net on the steps and returned to my cart.

Eric caught up with me. "I'll make sure it doesn't happen again."

"You can't promise that." I leaned on the steering wheel and closed my eyes. "I hate guns. I had a cousin killed by a random drive-by. Turns out they killed the wrong person. My aunt never got over his death and shot herself a year later."

He covered my hand with his. "I'm sorry. You've never said a word about the gun I carry."

"I pretend it doesn't exist." I forced a smile.

"Besides, you've never pointed it at me."

"I never will." He stepped back. "See you later?"

I nodded, pleased he liked me enough to seek my company. Next stop, Mags.

"Nope. Haven't seen or heard a thing." She straightened from her flower bed. "This community is dead and boring."

"Boring is good." I laughed. "Boring means nothing is disappearing."

"Give it time." She pointed her gardening spade at me. "The thief is biding her time, waiting to strike again. Lock up your valuables. Smart people can get around security cameras."

Living in an abandoned church didn't strike me as smart. "I'll take your advice. Don't talk to anyone about the cameras."

"Do you think everyone's blind? You can't miss those men in the trees."

"No, but I want them to forget the cameras are there. The only way we'll catch the thief is if she makes a mistake." And she would. They always did in the movies.

Caper came running, her gold and white coat covered with dirt and cobwebs. She hopped into the cart and dropped half a sheet of paper in my lap. It looked like half of a handwritten letter signed by…I could only make out the last three letters…red. I immediately thought of Red, but his real name was Dave. Besides, he'd capitalize his name, right?

I folded the letter and stuck it into my pocket to read later. "You, Caper, need a bath. Where have you been?"

When I arrived home, I saw the hole under my house. I groaned. Grammy hadn't told me her dog liked to dig. I bent down to scoop the dirt back into the hole and spotted the glimmer of silver.

Chapter Seven

I stretched out my arm, but couldn't reach what sparkled. Lying flat on my belly, I army-crawled toward the shining object and plucked a silver necklace from the dirt. Rolling over, I peered through a crack in my floor that looked strangely out of place. Definitely big enough for a necklace to fall through, but something seemed fishy about the way the floor lay. If this size crack existed, shouldn't I be able to see the light from my kitchen?

"Hey."

I startled, bumping my head. "Ow, Eric. Not nice."

"Sorry." He grabbed me around the ankles and pulled me from under the house. "What are you doing under there?"

"Look what I found." I held up the necklace, then sprang to my feet. "Caper brought me part of a letter. When I went to find the rest, I saw this. What gets me, though, is my floor seems a bit thick."

He plucked grass from my hair. "Explain,

please."

"I think someone put in an extra layer of flooring." I headed for the house. "Grab a crowbar. We're ripping it up."

"Hold on." He dug around in the back of his cart, returning with a crowbar. "I'll do it, so we can salvage some of it."

Good idea. I tended toward rambunctiousness when tackling construction projects. Following him into my house, I pointed to the spot over where I'd found the necklace.

The removal of one floorboard revealed a secret compartment. "It's empty." My shoulders sagged.

"Obviously it wasn't always empty." Eric replaced the board. "Maybe Ms. Rice kept her valuables here."

"Or maybe she is the thief. She could have made a copy of the keys to each of the houses, making access easy."

He laughed. "That old woman a thief? No, all she's guilty of is a sour personality and lack of ambition at improving this place."

"Maybe." I shrugged. "I'll mail her the necklace. She's probably looked everywhere for it." I removed the partial letter from my pocket and set it on the table. "There isn't much here, and the partial signature is likely hers."

He peered at the letter. "Can't read a thing. The last line is cut in half. Kind of looks like a list."

Disappointment filled me. I thought I'd found a clue to…something. "Oh, well." I stuck the letter in a drawer. Finding clues under my house would have been too easy. Still, it nagged at me. I decided to pay a visit to the community's know-it-all, Mags.

"Hold on a minute," Mags said when I told her about the necklace. She darted into her house, returning a minute later with a photograph. "This necklace?"

I studied the silver chain and cross around her neck. "That's it. Why didn't you mention it had gone missing?"

"Months ago. I thought I misplaced it." She slipped the photo into the pocket of her flowered coveralls. "The thief was hiding the stolen items right under our noses."

"Or you dropped the necklace and an animal dragged it under my house."

"Or that hidden space in your floor is to hide the goods." She raised her eyebrows. "I'm going with that idea. We need to visit Lenora."

"Who?"

"Lenora Rice. I'll get my purse." She returned from inside the house. "You'll have to drive. My license got suspended because of too many speeding tickets." She followed me to my Toyota Corolla. "Nice car."

"Thanks. I like her." Once inside I turned. "Where does she live?"

"I have no idea." She narrowed her eyes. "I thought you did."

"Why would you think that?"

"You took over her job. Didn't she leave a forwarding address?"

I rolled my eyes. "I'm not a post office, Mags." I climbed out of the car. "If I find out where she is now, I'll let you know."

"What a waste of my time." She stormed into her house.

I let her fume and went to look up Lenora Rice's address on the internet. It took a bit of searching, but I found her phone number, then searched using that. Half an hour later, I collected Mags and drove to a nearby town. No one answered the door at the small red brick home, so we sat on the front porch to wait.

"I don't think she's our thief," I said. "She brought up the robberies on my first day and told me to watch out for them."

"She might know something. What excuse are you going to use for us being here?"

Good question. I couldn't just blurt out that her having a hidden floor looked suspicious. "I'll, uh, wing it."

"Great plan." Her smirk said otherwise.

I stood as Lenora pulled into her driveway. She stopped the car and stared at us through the windshield. The absence of a smile led me to believe she wasn't happy to see us.

"The job too much for you?" She asked stepping onto the porch. "I thought it would be. You're too young."

I held up a hand to stop Mags from saying something she shouldn't. "It's actually going well, but there is something I could use your expertise with." *Think, CJ.*

"Well?" The woman's brow furrowed. "I ain't got all day."

"How's it feel to live in a house like this after a

tiny house?" Smooth.

"Much nicer." She narrowed her eyes. "You came all the way out here to ask me that?"

I sighed. "Why is there a secret space under the floor of my house? We found Mags' missing necklace in it."

"I kept my important papers and valuables there." She crossed her arms. "A safe can be stolen and broken into. They would've had to back up a truck and pulled the house away in order to steal those things. I told you things were disappearing. A person can't be too careful. As for the necklace, a raccoon most likely. They wear a mask for a reason, you know."

Made sense. "That's all." I stepped off the porch, then faced her. "Thank you for your time."

"You're a strange girl, you know that?"

"Hey." Mags stepped between us. "This so-called strange girl has already done more for the community than you did the whole five years you lived there. Why we've got—"

"Like what? The budget isn't big enough to do much of anything." Her lip curled.

"Oh, we're managing." I grabbed Mags' arm and led her back to the car. "Don't talk about the cameras, remember?"

"I know." She pulled free.

"You were about to tell her." I gave her "the look" my mother gave me when I lied as a child.

She plopped into the car like a sullen child. "I took up for you."

"Which I appreciate very much." I backed from the drive and turned the car toward home. I didn't know what I'd hoped to accomplish by visiting Lenora. She'd said the space was used for exactly what we thought.

"We should have broken into her house while she was gone," Mags said. "See if any of the missing items are in there."

"I don't think she's the thief. Can you picture her living in a decrepit church?"

"I guess not. We're back at square one."

"We never left." Eric was right. The thief had moved on.

After dropping Mags off at her home, I drove toward the path that led to the church. I needed something to do while I planned the next step in what was turning out to be no small caper. With rake in hand, I made my way down the path.

An hour later, I leaned on the rake, sweat pouring down my face, and surveyed the fruits of my labors. Not a single leaf or pile of debris remained. The wooden pews would need to be sanded and polished, which I'd leave in the capable hands of Roy. By the time the windows arrived, we'd be ready to turn this into a sanctuary for anyone seeking peace.

Out of the corner of my eye, I caught a flash of pink. I dropped the rake and sprinted down the path, following the sound of someone crashing through the underbrush. The occasional spot of pink told me I was on the right track. "Stop. Please. I just want to talk to you."

The person ahead of me increased the distance between us by the minute. I really needed to take up jogging if I wanted to pursue anyone on foot.

Panting, I balanced my hands on my knees and fought to catch my breath. The woman would be back.

The question I had now was…why watch me work? She couldn't possibly think the church was hers to live in again. I straightened and studied my surroundings. She had to be staying close by. Maybe she wasn't the thief, just a squatter. Maybe she was in need of help as I'd helped the Olson family. Again, more questions than I had answers.

Oh well, I… hmm. I slowly circled around in search of a path. Spying a broken branch on a bush, which I hoped I'd caused, I headed in that direction. Here I was in the woods, lost, with no weapon to protect myself from predators, two-legged or four. Way to go, CJ.

I did my best to follow broken branches, but since I wasn't the only living thing in the woods, I couldn't be sure of the right direction. Surely, I'd reach the campgrounds, community, or lake soon. Again, I wished for a radio to call Eric on. I'd make it a top priority when and if I arrived home.

Plopping on a log, I rested my elbows on my knees. No food or water. That realization made me suddenly very thirsty. How long had I been wandering around? It felt like hours. With a sigh, I heaved my tired body to my feet and continued my random plodding, blinking back tears.

Eric was right. I shouldn't put myself in danger. I couldn't cope. What an idiot. Who in their right mind chases after an alleged crook? Me, that's who. I swiped my hand across my eyes. Just keep walking. I had to come out somewhere. That became my mantra...wait, I recognized that tree. Darn it. I'd traveled in a big circle that didn't include the church or its path.

The tears started anew, and I leaned against a tree trunk.

Something hit me in the back of the head.

I fell to the ground as darkness overcame me.

Chapter Eight

I opened my eyes to a worried Eric leaning over me. "I'm so mad you haven't given me a radio yet."

His eyes widened. "What happened?" He helped me gently to a sitting position on a pile of decaying leaves.

"I got lost, then somebody hit me in the back of the head." I reached back, wincing as my fingers came in contact with a sensitive knot.

"Why were you all the way out here?" He knelt next to me and glanced around. "There's nothing here. Not even a hiking trail."

"Why are you?"

"I'm making my rounds, noticed the empty golf cart, came looking, and saw you on the ground. Almost gave me a heart attack. I thought you were dead." He glanced around us. "If you would have gone a hundred yards that way, you'd have come to the path."

I glared. "If you'd given me a radio, I could

have called you and told you I was lost. Then I wouldn't have been attacked."

"I'll give you one first thing when we get back. Why would someone attack you?"

"Because I was chasing the woman in pink." I explained how she'd been watching me clean the church. I pushed shakily to my feet. Nausea roiled in my stomach. "I might have a concussion." That's all I needed to say to spur him to action. Before I knew it, he'd scooped me into his arms and set off at a fast pace until we reached his cart—or side-by-side, I think I'd heard him call it. Anyway, it was like a golf cart on steroids.

After depositing me into the passenger seat, we sped toward the community. "Where are we going?"

"Number four."

Right. Amber was a nurse. I leaned back and closed my eyes, not opening them again until Eric carried me into her place.

After quickly explaining to Amber what had happened, he set me on a white leather loveseat and stepped back to let her work. She studied the knot on the back of my head and shone a light into my eyes. "Definitely a concussion. She should go to a doctor."

"I'm fine, or I will be once the nausea subsides." I shoved away the penlight. "That's unpleasant."

"Why would someone hit CJ?"

"Because she's nosy," Eric replied. "I can't get her to stay out of trouble to save my life."

Amber laughed. "Then stop trying. She's a

grown woman, and a stubborn one, if my assumption is correct."

"It is."

"The two of you can stop talking about me as if I'm not here and go find the person who hit me." I glared through spread fingers.

"I'll make coffee." Amber moved to her counter and inserted a pod into a bright red Keurig.

Eric sat on the love seat next to me. "You should have your head examined—I mean, checked."

"I've been told that before," I said, grinning. "I'll be fine."

He put his arm around me and placed my head in the crook of his shoulder. "You scared me, CJ. What do those initials stand for? I've been meaning to ask."

"Clarice Josephine." I shuddered. "I'm named after both of my grandmothers."

"I can see why you use your initials." His chest vibrated with silent laughter. "Still, it's a pretty name in an old-fashioned way."

Amber handed us each a cup of coffee, then after she'd made one for herself, dropped into the seat across from us. "I'm glad I'm not scheduled to work today."

"I'd have taken her to Urgent Care by force if you weren't here," Eric said.

"What in tarnation is going on in here?" Mags stepped inside and glared at each of us in turn. "I'm glad to see Eric has the sense not be here alone. What's wrong with you?"

"Someone hit her in the head out in the woods,"

Eric said. "I brought her here so Amber could look at her head."

"Hello, grandma." Amber raised her mug. "Coffee?"

"Not from you. It's probably spiked."

"No, but for you I'd make an exception. A little Kahlua might mellow you out." Amber raised the mug to her lips, her eyes twinkling.

"You know, I spent the last few years taking care of my grandmother while she suffered through dementia." I straightened, pulling out of Eric's hold. "It hurts my heart to see the two of you at odds with each other. You won't live forever, Mags."

She curled her lips. "No one will. When this girl straightens up, she'll be welcome back in my house."

"Yet here you are in mine." Amber laughed.

"You don't have the same scruples I do." Mags lifted her chin. "What do we do now to nab the person who hurt our CJ?" Her gaze switched to Eric.

"Violence in the park is my jurisdiction. *We* aren't doing anything." He placed his mug on a small corner table, then stood and unclipped the radio from his belt. "I've another one at the house. I'm always on channel two." He handed it to me. "Ready to go home?"

I glanced at Amber and Mags. "I think I'll stay awhile."

His eyes narrowed. "You three are going to make plans."

"Just talk." I smiled.

"Right." He shook his head and left, muttering

under his breath.

Mags took his place next to me. "Now that he's out of the way—"

"We shouldn't get involved," Amber said. "CJ might not be as lucky next time."

"Don't be a coward." Mags crossed her arms. "If we don't stop this person, someone else could be attacked."

"Or killed."

"That's why we need to track this person," I said. "It's our...my...responsibility to make sure the residents are safe. Since I have no sense of direction, I need someone to come with me. We'll start at the church." I stood on wobbly legs.

"You're in no condition to go anywhere." Amber shook her head. "But since you insist on such foolishness, you might need me to pick you up when you fall. Let me put on some shoes."

Hoping that a trek through the woods together would repair the rift between Amber and Mags, I stepped outside. I'd have to fetch my golf cart anyway, so might as well try to follow the woman in pink's path.

The three of us borrowed Roy's cart, promising to return it soon, then drove to where I'd left my cart. "Who's the tracker out of you two?"

"I am." Amber stepped down from where she'd hung onto the back of the cart. "I roamed these woods a lot as a child. My parents owned a house just down the road."

"You knew about the church and cross?"

"Sure. They unplugged the cross because it shone in people's windows and kept them awake.

The church wasn't used. Now that the tiny house community is here, maybe people will come back to it. It's a good idea you have, CJ."

Her kind words helped push the pain in my head aside almost as well as an aspirin would. "I can't stand back and let it fall down."

"I got married in that church," Mags said hardly above a whisper. "Hopefully, others will once it's repaired."

If I ever had the opportunity, I'd go. I couldn't imagine a more beautiful venue.

Amber stopped in front of the church and studied the ground. "It's clear which way you ran."

I glanced at two sets of footprints in the dirt. "It's getting back that had me confused."

She smiled. "Let's track the thief." Amber set off down the path, stopping every once in a while to study the ground. "Here's where you got lost. Your tracks go this way, and the others in the opposite direction."

"The woman was fast," I said in my defense. "I followed broken branches."

"Which a deer could have caused."

"Or a bear," Mags added.

I'd been lost in the woods where bears lived? "Is it safe for the community or the campground?" My eyes widened, causing the pain in my head to increase.

"They rarely come around. Bears are more afraid of you than you are of them," Amber said.

"I doubt it." I shuddered.

"Look." Mags plucked a patch of pink fabric from a thorny bush. "Too bad we don't have a hound dog."

Amber continued tracking until we came out of the woods on the edge of the campground. "She's either in one of those tents or she ran through here. Time to let Eric know he needs to search every tent."

"Too bad he won't know what he's looking for," I said. "Unless she's wearing a pink sweat suit with a hole in it, he won't know what she looks like."

Chapter Nine

"What is that boy up to?" Mags pointed to where Danny raced through the campground, a pink hoodie flapping behind him. "You don't think he's our mysterious woman, do you?"

I'd ring his neck if he played games with me. "How are you at running, Amber?"

"Pretty good." She took off like a rocket after the boy, while Mags and I followed at a much slower pace.

I wanted to start this day over. If I could, I wouldn't go chasing after the woman in pink, thus avoiding the knot on my head, which caused every placement of my foot to throb into my brain. I plopped onto the first picnic table we came to and rested my head on crossed arms.

The seat vibrated as Mags sat next to me. "Here."

I turned my head. In her hand lay three little rust-colored pills. "Ibuprofen?"

"Yep. You look as if you could use some, and I

never leave home without them. At my age, you never know when your body will protest at the most inconvenient time."

I swallowed them dry. "Thank you."

"It's a real good thing it ain't bedtime."

"Why's that?" I hid my face in the crook of my arms.

"Because you can't go to sleep for a while after a head injury. Everyone knows that." She remained silent for a couple of minutes, then said, "If we're going to be partners in this thing, you need to stop taking off on your own."

"I was cleaning out the church." I had no idea I'd chase someone through the woods and show my complete lack of direction in getting lost. "Next time I'll make sure to take two rakes and pick you up on my way."

"No need to get snippy." She tapped my shoulder. "There's Amber with that boy in tow."

I straightened as Amber stopped in front of us with a complaining Danny. "I told you I found the hoodie and was running to find Eric." He yanked his arm free of her grasp. "I'm not a thief, and I don't dress up in women's clothes. Eew. Who do you take me for?"

"A thief," Mags said.

"Where did you find it?" I narrowed my eyes. "You'd better tell the truth. I'm in no mood to play guessing games."

"I am telling the truth. I found this next to the water on the south side of the lake." He tossed the hoodie on the table. "I think your thief has changed clothes."

Wonderful. I didn't know what she looked like; now I wouldn't recognize her by the bright pink. She could be any one of the campers strolling by us for all I knew. "I'm ready to go home." I turned on the radio I'd clipped onto my waistband earlier and dialed Eric. "I'm in the campground. Can you come and get me?"

"Be there in five."

"You said I could help, CJ." A painful expression wafted across Danny's face. "That's all I was doing."

"It's okay." I leaned my elbow on the table and rested my head in my hand. I stared at the sunset kissing the lake. My stomach growled, reminding me I hadn't eaten in a few hours. "Anyone have any food?"

They shook their heads. "I can go grab some burgers and meet you at your house," Amber offered. "Grandma?"

"Plain old cheeseburger, hold the onions. As if you haven't ordered for me a hundred times." Mags rolled her eyes.

Amber was gracious enough to offer to pick one up for Danny, but he declined, saying he needed to get home before his mother started to worry. He darted away.

"I'll meet you at your place." Amber set off at a jog for her house.

"She ran track in high school," Mags explained. "She goes for a jog around the lake when time permits."

"You ought to be nicer to her. She's wonderful."

A sly smile spread across her face. "My way is

70

more fun and keeps her on her toes."

"You are a wicked woman." I stood as Eric pulled up in his cart.

"You okay?" Worry creased his face.

"I'm exhausted and starving." I climbed into the front seat, leaving the back for Mags. "Amber went to fetch us all burgers."

"Awesome."

As he drove us to my place, I told him about Danny finding the hoodie. "Do you think he's telling the truth?"

"I do." Eric helped me to the picnic table in front of my house, then let Caper out to join us and do her business. "It wouldn't make sense for him to try and fool us. We'd already caught him once."

I shrugged. "We're starting all over. Do you know whether the police have found out anything?"

He sat beside me. "They're as clueless as we are."

"That's not a surprise," Mags said. "Incompetent describes them very well. I told you once, and I'll tell you again, it's up to us to stop this thief."

"Nothing has disappeared in a few days," Eric said. "If not for CJ's mishap, I'd think they'd moved on."

"Have you questioned the campers? Maybe they've lost things and think them misplaced." I gazed toward the lake. "The way the campers come and go, they might not realize they're missing anything until they get home."

"That's a good point." He grinned at me. "I've already got Robinson making a list of all the campers in and out in the last month. Great minds think alike."

"I should have known you'd think of it." I leaned my head on his shoulder. After all, he was a trained park ranger and not an idiot by any means.

"While we wait for my infernally slow granddaughter," Mags said, "why don't we go over what we do know about the thief. Do you have paper in your house?"

"There's a notepad and pen in the drawer to the right of the sink. Hey, my headache is subsiding a bit." Good. I might be able to think.

Mags returned with the paper and sat across from us. "Female."

Eric chuckled. "Right down to business. Change that to suspected female. We don't know for sure."

"Thin, not too tall," I added. "Which leaves me to believe it's a young person or a woman. Not a man." I cut him a sideways glance.

"I agree, but we can't jump to conclusions." Eric nodded. "If we do, we miss things."

Mags put a question mark next to female. "Anything else?"

I frowned. "That's all we know." My heart sank. "Practically nothing."

"We know they have to be living somewhere close," Eric said. "This person is like a phantom, here and there, coming in and out of sight. We wouldn't spot them this often if they weren't close. The trick is finding them."

I had a feeling the culprit was right under our eyes, but we were too blind to see them. "Oh, good. The food has arrived."

Amber parked in front of the house and approached us with four bags, handing each of us our order. I couldn't help but wonder how she knew how Eric liked his burger and squelched down the flicker of jealousy trying to ignite.

"Oh, a list." Amber sat next to Mags and glanced at the page. "If Danny found the hoodie next to the lake's shore, we should try to track the thief from that spot. I just happen to have a flashlight in my glove compartment."

"I've one." Eric unwrapped a juicy burger slathered in barbeque sauce. Definitely not something ordered at random.

I sighed. "I've one in my cart which is at the head of the path near the church. I need to collect my cart anyway."

"Okay." Mags gave a definitive nod. "We have a plan. No telling where it will lead, but at least we have one."

After supper, the four of us, with Caper in my lap, drove to the south side of the lake and stared at a myriad of footprints. "This is pointless." I sighed.

"Not necessarily." Amber climbed from the cart. "All I have to do is find the prints that match the ones we followed in the woods and you found at Mags' place. Then we have a starting spot."

Appreciation flickered across Eric's face, sending my heart plummeting. Of course, he'd be interested in a woman like Amber. What man wouldn't? Sure, he said he enjoyed my company, but for how long? The more time he spent with Amber, the less he'd want to spend with shy, silly, awkward me.

"I found them, and they head straight for camp." Amber's teeth flashed in the glow of her flashlight. "Let's go."

The south end of the lake hadn't been cleared for swimming, camping, or much of anything, and the going was slow. Fatigue coated my limbs.

Eric slowed his pace and slipped his arm around my waist. "Want to rest here? We can come back and get you."

"I don't ever want to be alone in the woods again." I peered into his face, unable to read his expression in the dark. "You go on ahead with Amber, and I'll hang back with Mags."

"Okay. Don't dawdle too much." He jogged to catch up with Amber.

I sighed as the silhouettes of two strong, attractive people pulled ahead of us. Here I was at the age of twenty-six plodding along with an eighty-year-old.

Mags rested her hand on my shoulder. "Don't fret. You'll be able to keep up with them in a day or two. You mustn't push yourself."

"I know." I sighed again. Her words made sense but didn't make me feel any better.

We caught up to the other two on the edge of the campground. Caper, who usually bounded around our feet enough to be a nuisance, sat still, ears erect, and stared at the walls of a tent. A lantern outlined two silhouettes in the canvas. Loud words rose in the night.

"If you don't do what you're told, you'll regret it," a woman said.

"Right. I'm shaking in my boots," a man said.

"Go ahead and shoot me. I'm tired of your games."

Eric glanced over his shoulder at me, eyes wide, and motioned for us to remain still. Crouching, he moved closer to the tent.

Caper barked.

The man cursed.

A shot rang out.

One of the bodies fell with a thud.

Footsteps pounded away.

Chapter Ten

"Amber, see to the person inside, I'm going after the runner." Eric shot around the tent.

Mags and I followed Amber into the tent. A man in faded blue jeans and a long sleeve shirt, faded to a nondescript color, held a hand over his bleeding right arm. Thank goodness he hadn't been shot dead.

"What do y'all want?" The man glared. "Get me a doctor instead of standing there staring."

"I'm a nurse." Amber bent over him, pulling his hand away. "Just a graze. If you have something clean I can bandage your wound with, we'll have someone drive you to the hospital."

"I ain't going to no hospital for nothing more than a bug bite."

"Who shot you?" I asked. "Sounded like a woman threatened you before she shot."

"My girlfriend. It ain't none of your business, but she's mad because I won't put a ring on her finger. That woman has enough jewelry as it is."

"Sir, we'll have to report this to the police. All gun wounds have to be noted." Something else I'd heard in one of the television crime shows I liked to watch.

"You'll have to force me."

Eric ducked into the tent. "Fine. We'll tie you up and drag you to the station, or we can stand guard over you until the police arrive." He glanced at us three women. "She got away, and I called the police."

I wanted to ask whether it was our thief but figured the surly man on the floor didn't need to know our business any more than he wanted us to know his. "What's your name?"

"None of Your Business, the Third."

I wanted to shoot him myself. Instead, I aimed my glare at him until he fidgeted. Biting back a smile, I stepped out of the tent as sirens wailed in the distance.

Two squad cars stopped in front of the tent, Milton and Perk getting out of one, and a man in a dress shirt and tie out of the other. Milton's lip curled. "Detective Davis, this is Miss Turley, who always seems to be where there's trouble."

The handsome detective smiled. "Pleased to meet you, ma'am." He parted the tent flap and stepped inside.

I didn't know law enforcement could look that good outside of Hollywood.

"Put your eyes back in your head," Mags said, joining me. "You'll embarrass yourself. It must be the knock on your head that's got you wonky. Speaking of...you need to report that you were attacked."

"Attacked?" Detective Davis poked his head out of the tent.

Lord, I hope he hadn't heard the rest of Mags' statement. "Someone hit me in the back of the head earlier today when I was lost in the woods."

He nodded. "I'll be out to take your statement when I finish up in here." The flap closed.

Instead, Milton came out and told me to sit at the concrete picnic table. "You should have called this in when it happened."

"I've been busy."

"Doing what? Your job can't be so hard that you can't pick up the phone."

"It isn't." I crossed my arms. "I got lost in the woods, got attacked, then Eric found me, and we tried to find out who hit me. That's all of the story until we reached here, heard the argument, then the gunshot. The man inside said his girlfriend took aim over the lack of a ring on her finger."

"That's what he says." Milton wrote down what I'd told him. "Really do try to stay out of trouble, won't you?"

"Why? Am I making your job too hard?"

He scowled and rejoined the other officers as an ambulance arrived, absent lights whirling or siren. I guess they'd been told the man wasn't seriously injured. After they led the sour-faced man from the tent, Eric and Amber joined Mags and me at the table.

"Do you feel like walking back or do you want me to get the cart and come get you?"

"I'm fine." I stood.

"Me too. Can't let you people think I'm too old to keep up." Mags started back the way we'd come.

Amber laughed. "I really do love that feisty old woman."

Me too.

~

The next morning I sat outside with my coffee, headache barely bothering me, and waited for Roy to show up and get his list of chores for the day. The men installing the cameras had finished and gone. Pride welled up in me for all I'd done to improve the community in the short time I'd been there. The owner had even sent me a job-well-done email and a fifty cent an hour raise. Life was good at Heavenly Acres except for the nagging problem of a thief.

I grinned as Eric stopped his side-by-side. "Good morning."

"Good morning." He hopped down. "Robinson said several of the previous campers told him they'd misplaced things. Nothing big, things that make camp life a bit easier." He grinned. "Things that would help someone live in the woods."

"So our thief set him- or herself up before stealing from the tiny houses."

"It looks that way. Got any more coffee?"

"Sure do." I headed into the house, returning with my cup refilled and a fresh one for him. "I'd offer you some cake, but I ate it."

"Had breakfast, thanks." He smiled across the table at me. "I'm glad to see you feeling better after yesterday's adventure."

"Good thing since the barbeque is tomorrow." I

could get used to morning coffee with him.

Roy pulled up and I handed him the list the day's jobs. He perused it. "Church windows will arrive today. Want me to make that top priority?"

"Don't you have them being installed?"

"Yep, but I'll want to supervise and make sure they do a good job."

I laughed. "Yes, make it a priority. A faucet that's been leaking in one of the rentals for a week can wait another day if it needs to." Especially since I didn't have anyone needing to move in.

"Tammy said she'll be by to make sure everything's on the list for tomorrow. Ranger." He nodded at Eric before driving off.

"I don't think he's ever gotten over the fact I hauled his son to the police station." Eric drained the last of his coffee. "Keep your radio with you." He tossed me a wink and climbed back into his vehicle.

That was my cue to start the day. I needed to make sure the area was ready for tomorrow's barbecue and also go through the remaining rentals. Summer would bring people wanting to enjoy the lake from a patio rather than a tent.

The large common area and gazebo sat in the center of the community with the tiny houses extending down each side. The freshly mowed grass invited blankets and lawn chairs. Eric had already moved his large grill into the gazebo. Nothing for me to do there.

Mags flagged me down as I approached her house. "Heard a rumor there was movement in the furthest house last night. Danny said he saw a light flicker."

"Why didn't he tell me?"

"Because I told him I would." Her brow furrowed.

"What were the two of you doing up so late?"

"Patrolling." She shook her head. "Don't you pay any attention to what goes on around you?"

"Apparently not." I'd gone straight to bed. "Hop in. We'll check it out together."

"Have Eric meet us there so we don't get whacked." She climbed up.

I handed her the radio and drove to house twenty while she called for backup. Since it didn't appear as if anyone was inside, I pushed open the door that had been jimmied.

We'd found the new home of our thief. Sleeping bag, propane lantern, cookstove—everything a person needed who didn't have electricity. Yep, there were the pink sweat pants. Our thief wore something new.

"Bingo."

I yelped and spun around. "Not nice, Mags. You know I'm a little jumpy after yesterday."

"Sorry." She shrugged and pulled a yellow tube from her pocket.

Footsteps sounded.

Mags whirled.

A loud pop, an electric current, and Eric jerked, falling to the floor like a beached fish.

"Mags!" I shot her a dirty look and knelt next to Eric.

"First time I've used that thing. I wasn't sure it worked. He'll come to in a few seconds."

From the glare in Eric's eyes, he was fully alert and furious. When the shock wore off, he rose to shaky feet and yanked the Taser from Mags' hand. "You're a danger to society."

"Only in intense circumstances. Give that back. We might need it."

"I'll give it back when I'm not mad." He stepped around us and studied the camping items. "Too bad the cameras weren't turned on until this morning. We would have had a face."

"I'll get Roy to clear this out and fix the door," I said. "Maybe the police can get fingerprints?"

"Maybe. I'll give them a call. Again." With another glare at Mags, he stepped outside, dropping her Taser in the grass.

"Guess he'll be upset for a while." Mags retrieved her Taser and slipped it back into her pocket.

Laughter overtook me and I wrapped my arms around my middle, snorting. Tears ran down my face. I held up my hand as the other two stared at me.

"She's lost her mind," Mags said, glancing up at Eric.

"CJ?"

"I'm…fine." I took a deep breath, but another glance at the shock and worry on their faces started me up again. I still giggled when Milton and Perk arrived.

"What's wrong with her?" Milton asked.

"She get attacked again?" Perk frowned.

"No." Mags shook her head. "The stress is too much for her."

I leaned against the house to catch my breath. "Everything is inside. We didn't touch anything."

The officers nodded, then entered the house. I exhaled long and slow, finally regaining my composure. "I needed that laugh."

Eric's eyes widened. "If I thought you'd react that way again, I'd have Mags zap me a second time." He rubbed his side. "That hurt though."

"Y'all are a bunch of crazies," Milton said from the small porch. "Zapping each other for the sake of laughter. We're closing this house off as a crime scene until we get to the bottom of this. Have you considered a Neighborhood Watch?"

"Got one," Mags said, squaring her shoulders. "I'm the head of the organization around here."

"Heaven help us all." He opened the trunk of the squad car and pulled out a roll of yellow tape. While Perk took pictures, Milton secured the scene.

"How long?" I asked. "I'm going to need this house soon."

"Can't say," Perk answered. "We'll try to get to it quickly."

That didn't sound promising for the foreseeable future. "This thief stays one step ahead of us."

"But those steps are getting smaller." Eric grinned. "She's running out of places to hide."

I shook my head. "This doesn't make sense. She or he had to know they'd be discovered. What if this is only a red herring?"

"A fish?" Mags' eyes widened.

"A false clue."

Eric pressed his lips together. "That makes sense, kind of. We've not found a single stolen item at either place where the person supposedly camped." He stepped into the drive and looked toward the other houses. "I'm beginning to think our thief is part of the community."

"We'll study everyone at the barbeque tomorrow." Maybe we'd find a clue.

Chapter Eleven

The afternoon of the barbeque donned us with partial clouds and a slight breeze. Perfect weather for an outdoor gathering. The aroma of roasting meat drifted from the grill. The sound of laughing children filled the air as families arrived, some from the nearby campground, and headed off for a game of tag. I'd left the nearest empty rental unlocked and opened for any curious future tenants, and already had a couple of promising prospects.

"You did good, kid." Mags handed me a cold bottle of water. "Now to find us a thief."

"Let's enjoy the day first, all right?" Out of the corner of my eye, I spotted the yellow crime-scene tape waving in the distance, the one sore spot to an otherwise beautiful day. Milton would probably leave it there longer than necessary just to spite me.

"Of course, but it doesn't hurt to keep our eyes and ears ready to spot trouble."

No, it didn't, and while I intended to enjoy myself, I'd also mingle. "Lenora is here."

"Scoping out the improvements, no doubt. I'll go see how jealous she is." Mags ambled to where the other woman stood under a tree.

Amber took her place at my side. "My grandmother thrives on gossip and drama."

I smiled. "She does like to know everyone's business."

"Eric said the man shot in the camp, Ronnie Ward, refused to press charges on the woman who shot him."

"A dead end then, unless you managed to find out the woman's name?" I cast her a hopeful glance.

"Nope, and if Eric knows, he isn't saying. Did Mags really tase him?" She grinned. "I would've loved to have seen that."

"She did." I laughed. "He was spitting nails when he got to his feet."

Eric shouted out that the ribs were done, and Amber and I followed the crowd, grabbing some sturdy disposable plates on the way. I knew he'd slow cooked them overnight before tossing them on the grill, and I couldn't wait to fill my plate.

My mouth watering, I sat at the table in front of my house and dug into a sweet and spicy rib. I groaned and wiped my mouth on a napkin as Mags led Lenora over. "Hey."

"The place looks the same." Lenora sat. "I thought you made improvements."

"Mostly on the inside. It's nice having a handyman." Did she come to criticize?

"At the expense of giving up a rental?" She pursed her lips. "You're supposed to make a profit."

"We are." I leaned back and crossed my arms.

"Having the houses in good condition means people will want to rent or purchase more. We might even have a waiting list one day."

She shrugged. "I guess we have different ways of making money."

Marcy Wilson, the renter from number ten, strolled past us laughing with Red Jones. She cast us a quick glance, seeming to settle her gaze on Lenora, then nodded and moved on.

"Do you know her?" I asked.

Lenora turned. "She rented for a while last year. Why?" She faced me and narrowed her eyes.

"Just curious. Do you get a lot of repeat tenants?"

"Some." She stuck a plastic fork into the pasta salad on her plate. "It's a good vacation spot, good view of the lake."

Mags, who had remained suspiciously quiet so far, spoke up. "She's fixing the church and the cross too."

"That cross is a menace. You'll have to close your blinds at night."

"I don't mind," I said. "It has an off and on switch or can be powered by solar. It will be inspiring."

"More wasteful improvements," she scoffed, "that don't need to be made. The owner is going to be irate at the way you toss away his money."

"Have you ever met him?"

"No. We did everything over email." Her brow furrowed. "I always thought that strange."

We agreed on something. "So far, the owner has been open to my improvements."

Eric and Amber joined us. The niggling bit of jealousy rose again. How silly could I possibly be? I had no claim on the man although I wouldn't mind calling him mine.

"Glad you could join us, Ms. Rice," he said. "How's it feel to be back?"

"Less stressful."

"Still a woman of few words." He laughed and dug into his ribs. "Everyone seems to be having a good time, CJ. Good job."

"Probably the food." I smiled, the familiar flush rising as it usually did when he was near.

Mags pushed her empty plate to the side and crossed her arms. "For someone who hated it here, I'm surprised you came, Lenora. How did you find out about this get-together?"

The woman paled. "Someone must have mentioned it."

"You still keep in touch with the residents?" Mags raised an eyebrow.

"I probably heard it in town while running errands." The woman's body language matched Mags'. "Why all the questions, you nosy old woman?"

"Hey, that's my grandmother you're calling names." Amber's eyes flashed. "No one can do that but me."

"I suspect an ulterior motive for you being here." Mags gave a sly smile. "Jealousy?"

"The people around here are as weird as always." Lenora stood and stomped away, leaving her half-eaten food on the table.

"Something's not right with that woman." Mags

placed Lenora's plate on top of hers. "If she didn't have that slight limp, I might think she was the thief."

Limp? I hadn't noticed before. I stared after Lenora, noting the way she hitched slightly on her left foot. Definitely not our thief. Maybe we'd find the culprit by process of elimination. "The thief has a smooth walk, not too long of a stride."

Eric looked impressed. "Good eye." His gaze roamed the crowd. "Fits a lot of the people here, but some we can rule out. The bigger men, of course, the plumper women."

"Rules me out." Mags laughed and patted her stomach.

"Actually, you fit the profile," he said. "Small, with a confident stride."

"But I can't run worth a lick, and you know it." She frowned.

"Okay, you aren't the thief." He winked at her.

I went inside and grabbed the notepad we'd jotted characteristics on before and scribbled down some thoughts. I wrote down Red Jones and put an X through his name, then did the same with Lenora. In another row, I added Amber's name, and Marcy from number ten.

"Why's my name on this side?" Amber's eyes widened. "That's the suspect side."

"No offense, but you match the profile." I tapped the pen against my teeth and surveyed the crowd. Bob Guide, small and wiry, was written under Marcy's name. So was Danny and his mother, Tammy.

"You're writing down people you know didn't

steal anything." Amber's voice hardened.

"We don't know a whole lot at this point. Don't take offense; just roll with it. I'm only brainstorming." I continued watching the crowd.

"I think she protests too much," Mags said, raising both eyebrows. "Nursing school was expensive. Maybe you're stealing to pay off debt."

"Stop accusing each other," Eric said. "I see what CJ is doing. She'll cross your name off soon enough."

"I wish I knew the names of the campers," I said. "Any of them been hanging around for a while?"

Eric shook his head. "Not as long as the theft has been going on. I still think it's one of the tiny house residents. It could be someone from town, but that's a stretch. Could be why they felt like they needed to camp out."

"I thought we determined that was a ploy." I faced him.

"Can't say for sure one way or the other."

"Hmm." I wrote down the newlyweds from number two, Mark and Linda Boyles; Lucy Flower, the single mom from number six; and also Dave Lincoln in number three. I thought him too tall, but figured we could rule him out with a few subtle questions.

"I need to visit all the houses again," I said. "I'll say I'd like to get to know my residents better, ask some questions to start marking off more of these names." I studied Amber with a sharp eye. The thief was a fast runner. Amber had run track in high school.

"Stop looking at me as if I'm a crook." She shot to her feet. "I thought we were becoming friends, CJ." She gathered up the empty plates and strode to a nearby trashcan.

"She isn't the thief," Eric said.

"She fits."

"So do you."

I glared at him, then wrote my name on the suspect side. "I'm pretty sure we can cross my name off before we can hers."

I did feel bad about suspecting her and hoped I wasn't ruining a friendship because of jealousy. Finding the thief required a clear head and decisive thinking. I'd concentrate on clearing her name first.

Finished with lunch, I excused myself and chose to mingle. I didn't know the questions I wanted to ask yet, so I simply smiled, nodded, and hoped to stumble into an interesting conversation. A quick glance toward my house showed Eric and Mags watching me with interest. Probably hoping I'd mess up somehow.

That wasn't fair. Amber was family and friend to them. I knew she wasn't the thief and put an X through her name before heading to her house.

"I'm sorry." I stood in her open doorway.

"Me too." She rushed to me and grabbed me in a hug. "I see why you wrote my name down. I'm a good runner, but I am too tall."

I stepped back. She was right. The thief was only a few inches taller than I was. Amber was a good five or six inches. "Want to hang out with me tonight in hopes we see something?"

"Sure. I'll bring wine." She smiled. "I'll be at

your place at ten wearing black."

I laughed, looking forward to another adventure. "What about Mags?"

"She's out every night doing her neighborhood watch. I keep an eye on her in case she gets into trouble. We'll have to be careful she doesn't see us or she'll think we're spying on her." She glanced at her phone. "I work tomorrow, but if I'm in bed by midnight, I'll be alright."

So we needed to avoid Mags, Danny, and Eric while eavesdropping outside houses and hoping to spot a thief. Got it. "See you tonight." I turned to leave, catching sight of something blue out of the corner of my eye. "Someone's outside listening." I darted out the door and around the house.

No one stood there, but I knew what I'd seen. I planted my fists on my hips and studied the crowd. A lot of people wore blue. Darn it. Whoever listened would know Amber and I would be out that night.

"Things just got a lot more interesting," she said.

Chapter Twelve

We hadn't discovered any clue worth pursuing outside Amber's house, and now we hunkered in the bushes, sipping wine, waiting for something to happen. Only fifteen minutes into our stakeout and my thighs burned. I tried shifting to a more comfortable crouch.

"Stop fidgeting," Amber hissed. "You're rustling the bush."

"Maybe someone will think I'm a large raccoon." I moved to a kneeling position.

"If so, they might shoot you. Be still."

Boredom quickly set in. I wasn't much of a wine drinker and declined a second glass. Maybe if I'd had another, I wouldn't care that nothing happened. Wait. I sat up straighter. "Look," I whispered.

"That's Mags."

I peered closer. Oh, right. I sighed and watched as the older woman strolled the community with no pretense of secrecy as she whistled softly. Maybe she had the right idea. Another form stepped from the shadows, more sinister and secretive than Mags. "She's being followed. Come on."

Staying low, I followed the one following Mags while Amber stayed behind me. It was up to us to keep the old woman safe.

Mags stopped near the crime scene tape and shined her flashlight around the ground. What was she looking for that the police missed? She had to have a purpose for investigating that house again.

The stranger stopped behind a large tree and watched her. The person didn't wear a bright color; the black he or she wore enabled him to melt into the darkness. I hoped the security cameras could see more than we could.

Amber tapped me on the shoulder and pointed to our right. Another person in dark clothes stepped from between two of the rentals. This one entered house number three without knocking. Burglary or clandestine meeting? Did the widower, Dave Lincoln, have a girlfriend? I hadn't seen whether the person came from one of the houses or not.

"Maybe Eric's right about people from town coming here," I whispered.

Mags clicked off her flashlight and headed in our direction. I stepped back, snapping a twig under my foot.

She froze, the light flicking on. "Who's there?"

The shadowy figure didn't move. Were they waiting for Mags to get close enough to grab? I couldn't let that happen. I motioned for Amber to move behind the stranger. Then when I stepped out to greet Mags, she could keep them from running.

I waited until Amber got into position, then stepped from my hiding place. "It's me. Sorry if I scared you."

Mags shook her head. "Why didn't you just say so instead of skulking around? You almost gave me a heart attack."

"There's someone watching you," I whispered. "Amber's gonna stop them from running."

"Where?" Mags spun.

"Act natural. Follow me." I laughed, tossing my head back, doing a horrible job of acting as if everything were normal. My heart threatened to beat out of my chest despite my bravado. If the shadowy figure had evil intentions, not only Mags was in their path now.

"Have you been drinking?" Mags sniffed.

"I had one glass with Amber, yes."

"Don't let that girl be a bad influence on you."

"Even Jesus turned water into wine, but I'll be careful." My heart warmed knowing she cared that much about me.

We were nearing the person's hiding place. A sheen of perspiration broke out on my upper lip. I was definitely not brave. We passed the tree. No sign of anyone, not even Amber.

"Where is she?" Mags glanced around. "The thief took her."

"We would have heard a scuffle." Instead, other than our voices, the night was eerily silent. "Let's wake up Eric to help us find her."

"No need."

I yelped and whirled. "Where did you come from?"

Eric's teeth flashed. "I've been following you from the beginning."

"Did you see where Amber went?"

His smile faded. "No, but she can't have gone far. No cars have left here, and she isn't one to be taken without making some noise. Stay close and follow me."

Follow him where? We'd already covered the community. I kept my mouth shut and did as I was told.

Mags shuffled after us, her steps dragging. If it wasn't her granddaughter missing, she probably would have gone home and let us do the searching. I linked my arm through hers to help her along.

"Psst." Amber peered over a garbage can in the green area.

"Thank the Lord." Mags sighed. "Where have you been? You've had us worried sick."

"Shh." She motioned for us to follow, then stopped next to house number six. "Just wait and watch."

Soon someone stepped around the corner of number seven and darted for the porch of the house we hid behind. Eric stepped out. "Stop."

The figure yelped. "I live here."

"It's Lucy's oldest," Amber said.

"What are you doing out here?" Eric crossed his arms. "Do you know what time it is?"

"Yes." She pushed back the hood of her jacket. "I followed my mom to see where she goes a couple times a week. She's at that old man's house. Gross."

"You did more than look for your mother," Amber said. "I've been following you. Why were you watching Mags for so long?"

"I thought she was the thief Danny told me about."

I groaned. He shouldn't be talking to anyone. This girl could very well be the thief. "What's your name?"

"Rose Flower. Corny, I know, but Mom named us all after plants. My poor brother is named Briar. Can you imagine?"

I could, actually. Clarice Josephine wasn't exactly a popular name. "How old are you?"

"Almost thirteen." Her eyes widened. "I'm old enough to watch over my brother and sisters when my mother isn't home."

"Only if you actually stay at home," Eric added. "You can't be wandering around at night. It isn't safe for a young girl."

"What's wrong?" Lucy Flower ran toward us. "Are the kids okay?"

"We're fine, Mom." Rose rolled her eyes.

"Your daughter was out roaming around," Eric said. "With a thief on the loose, it isn't safe."

"She said she was looking for you," I added, not liking the fact the woman left her children alone at night to spend time with a man. He ought to come to her place, not that there would be much room, or privacy, in a tiny house full of children.

"Rose, go in the house." Lucy motioned her head. When her daughter obeyed, she said, "A thief?"

"Yes, ma'am." Eric nodded. "Things have been disappearing around here for about a month."

"Is it Rose? She's been caught shoplifting

before." She cast a worried glance in the direction her daughter had gone. "I thought she was past that."

"We don't know who the thief is," I said. It didn't look good that the girl had been caught snooping and had a past of stealing. "We'd like to ask her some questions in the morning."

"You can ask her now." She pushed the door open. "Rose, come back out here."

"I'm taking Mags home," Amber said. "She's beat."

"Speak for yourself." Mags glowered.

"Okay, I'm tired."

"That's more like it." Mags followed Amber away.

A sullen Rose rejoined us. "What?"

"Watch the tone." Lucy crossed her arms. "Have you been stealing from the people of this community?"

"No." Her eyes widened as she shook her head, hair flying around her face.

"Then why are you out so late? Don't give me that cockamamie story about following me. You knew where I was."

She muttered.

"Speak up."

"I snuck out to see Danny."

"I told you that boy was too old for you. You're not even thirteen yet." Lucy turned to me. "Will you have a word with his parents?"

"I will." A sixteen-year-old boy had no business sneaking around with a girl Rose's age.

Rose took a deep breath. "There's no reason to.

He doesn't know I'm stalking him. I saw him out my window one night and decided to follow him. I think he's cute, but he doesn't notice me." Her eyes shimmered. "You might want to ask him what he's doing sneaking around every night, dressed in black, peeking in windows."

Chapter Thirteen

I pulled up to the Olson house right after my morning coffee. When Roy appeared, I asked to speak to Danny.

"I've heard you've been peeking in windows," I said the moment he appeared.

Danny frowned. "I'm part of the neighborhood watch. I'm supposed to be patrolling."

"You're not old enough to be part of any such thing," Roy said. "Are you peeking in windows or not?"

"Yes. I'm trying to find the thief. I figured if I saw one of the stolen items in someone's house, we'd catch 'em."

A sixteen-year-old's reasoning didn't always make sense. "Your being out-and-about has caused a young girl to do the same."

"Rose? She's a stalker? I can't believe I haven't seen her following me." He dropped onto the top step. "What she does isn't my fault. Maybe she's the thief."

I hadn't discarded the idea. "I think it best you leave the nighttime snooping to the grown-ups."

"Mags needs someone watching out for her." He glanced up at his step-father. "She's old, and she hasn't been feeling well since the barbeque."

Which would explain her not being her usual talkative self. I'd check on her as soon as I was done here.

"Something else to leave to the adults," Roy said. "I don't want to hear another word about it, or I'm going to keep you so busy this summer you won't be able to do anything at night but sleep."

Danny's face darkened, and he ducked his head. "Fine."

Sirens wailed at the entrance to the community. I excused myself and sped in that direction, my heart in my throat. I arrived to see Mags being carried on a gurney from her house and Amber standing by.

"What happened?" I slid from the golf cart.

"Stomach pains, sweating...I found her curled up on the floor and called the ambulance." She sniffed.

"Danny said she hasn't felt well since the barbeque."

"Before then." Amber faced me. "She's been quiet the last few days. When I asked her, she said she thought she might have caught a stomach bug."

"You don't think so?" My eyes widened.

"I have a hunch." She gripped my arm. "Call Eric. Explain that I've gone with Mags to the hospital. She has a coffee mug she reuses every day, even brings it outside with her when she works in her flower bed. Find it, and have Eric take it to the police."

"Poison? Doesn't she wash her mug?"

"Barely rinses it. Only uses it for coffee and says dish soap ruins the taste. You know how she is. Will you do it?"

I nodded. "Right away. Go." I unclipped the radio from my waistband as she climbed into the ambulance.

"Come to Mags' quick."

"On my way."

During the short-radio conversation, I stepped into the overcrowded tiny house and couldn't help but wonder how the paramedics fit inside to take Mags out. I averted my eyes from the one clear spot on the floor where she must have fallen and moved to the kitchen sink. As in my house, the single sink barely held a meal's worth of dishes. On the drainboard rested a bright yellow coffee mug adorned with painted lady bugs. I'd seen it in Mags' hand plenty of times.

I searched the cupboards for something to put it in, then gingerly lifted it between my fingers and dropped it into a paper sack with handles, the kind a person gets when shopping at fancy boutiques. Eric pulled up in his truck as I exited the house.

"Get in." He shoved open the passenger door.

"Can we go to the hospital after the police station?" I set the bag on the floor and settled into my seat, clicking the seatbelt into place.

"You bet." He sped toward the freeway. "Amber thinks Mags is poisoned?"

I nodded. "As a nurse, she must have recognized

the symptoms." Fear curdled in my stomach. What if it was too late for treatment? The community wouldn't be the same without Mags. I said a quick prayer for her recovery.

Eric put his hand over mine. "I know what you're thinking. She'll be fine. Mags is a tough old bird."

"I know."

We rode in silence until we reached the police station. I hoped Milton would take us seriously and send the mug to the lab. I grabbed the bag and followed Eric inside.

"We need to speak with Detective Davis." Eric approached the reception desk. "It's important. I'm Eric Drake."

Oh, good. Maybe we wouldn't have to deal with Milton at all.

The middle-aged woman nodded, noting the patch on Eric's ranger shirt, and pressed a button on her headset. "An Eric Drake and a woman are here to see you, sir. Said it's important." She nodded. "He'll be right out. Have a seat."

I fidgeted, leaning forward to look down the hall, picking up and setting down the bag until Eric groaned and put a hand on my shoulder. "Sorry. What's taking him so long?"

"It's been ten minutes. He's busy."

I sighed, then leaped to my feet as the detective strolled toward us. "Come into my office." He motioned for us to follow him, then took a seat behind his desk. He folded his hands on top of a calendar desk blotter filled with notes. "What's up?"

"Amber Jones, the granddaughter of Mags Snyder, called for an ambulance this morning when she found Mags curled up on the floor. Amber, a nurse, thinks someone might have poisoned Mags and asked us to bring you this." I set the bag on his desk. "It's the mug Mags uses every day, all day. We'd like you to send it to the lab to be tested for poison."

He leaned back in his desk. "Have the doctors confirmed poison?"

"No, but Amber is a nurse."

He smiled, then glanced at Eric. "What do you think?"

"I think it's worth looking into. A lot of shady things have been happening at Heavenly Acres. With this only a few days after someone attacked CJ, I tend to lean on the side of caution."

Detective Davis nodded. "I'll take care of it, and I'll send the officers to Ms. Snyder's home."

I groaned, causing both men to laugh. "Officer Milton is hard to take."

Davis glanced over my shoulder and grinned. "He is."

A throat cleared behind me. "I could say the same about you, Miss Turley."

I turned and smiled at Milton. "Good morning."

"Hmph." He crossed his arms. "More trouble at the tiny houses?"

Davis nodded. "I'd like you and Perk to check things out. Let me know if I need to go. In the meantime, I'll take this mug to the lab and pay a visit to the alleged victim at Mercy General."

Dismissed, Eric and I headed for the hospital

and waited for news. Eric pulled out his cell phone and texted someone. "I let Amber know we're here."

He had her phone number? My shoulders slumped. Of course he did. I was the newcomer. They'd probably known each other for quite a while. To hide my emotions, I gazed out the window at a garden surrounded by crepe myrtle trees, a view designed to sooth troubled souls waiting as we were.

Amber arrived about thirty minutes later, Davis right after. "Arsenic poisoning. The doctor thinks she's been given slow doses over the last few days."

My hands clenched. "Can she be treated?"

"Yes, but she'll stay here for a few days to make sure she won't suffer any lingering problems." Amber collapsed into a chair. "We have to stop this person. Why Mags?"

Davis sat next to her. "Your grandmother is a nosy woman putting herself in situations she has no business getting into." He glanced at me. "Same as Miss Turley."

"CJ."

"Excuse me?"

"You might as well call me CJ. I have a feeling we're going to be seeing a lot of each other." I needed to find this thief, now attempted murderer, before someone actually died. Things had become personal.

"Stay out of it, Miss...CJ." Davis stood. "Ranger, you're going to have to keep these women out of trouble. I'd hate to arrest them for obstruction of justice."

"It'll be like herding cats, but I'll do my best." Eric smiled.

"It's not like I asked to be hit over the head, or Mags to get poisoned. The crook has brought the war to us." I narrowed my eyes. "We can't sit back and do nothing."

"You can, and you will." He gave me a stern glance, then strode out of the room to speak to Mags.

"I'll come get you when he's gone," Amber said, following the detective.

I hated waiting. I was a woman of action. "We need a plan. A trap to catch this person."

"Nope." Eric shook his head.

"We can't do nothing."

"Yep."

"Stop it." I'd do it without him. The determined glint in Amber's eyes spoke to me. She'd be my willing accomplice. I glared at Eric. "You're impossible."

"For wanting to keep you safe?" He raised his brows. "That isn't very nice of you."

"Oh, hush." I stepped into the hall and paced, my brain trying to come up with something foolproof.

Amber motioned to me from opened double doors. "You can come in now."

"Eric." I hurried after Amber, Eric on my heels. We entered Mags' room as Davis was leaving. I ignored the repeat warning he gave and rushed to her bedside.

"How are you feeling?" I took her hand.

"Like I could strangle someone." She raised red-rimmed eyes to me. "Try to kill me? We'll show them how tough I really am. When we find this person, I get first dibs at smacking them."

I laughed, glancing across the table at Amber and Eric. "I think she's going to be just fine."

"As soon as I get out of here." Mags tried to sit up, then fell back against the pillows. "Tomorrow will be a good time to get started."

"None of you paid any attention to the detective, did you?" Eric's eyes darted from me, to Amber, to Mags. "What if this person succeeds in killing one of you the next time?"

"Then the others take up the sword and persevere," Mags said. "If they wanted me dead, they would have given me a fatal dose or hit CJ harder. These are nothing more than scare tactics."

I agreed. There had been plenty of opportunities to kill one of us. I swallowed against a sudden dry throat. "Eric, you'll have to be our bodyguard, seeing as how you have a gun."

"Oh, no." He shook his head. "My job is to keep you out of trouble, not watch over you while you're in the middle of it."

All three of us women stared at him, not speaking or blinking until he squirmed. "Stop it. I'm serious." He crossed his arms, his jaw tightening. "Stare all you want. It won't change my mind."

"He's so cute thinking he can outwit three women." Mags laughed, then coughed. "Give in already, young man, I'm tired."

"She's right, you know." Amber grinned. "You can't resist us."

His eyes flashed. High spots of color appeared

on his cheeks. I almost felt sorry for him.

"It's our job to keep the community safe," I said, tilting my head.

"We aren't vigilantes," he argued, then his features softened. "Fine. But none of you do anything without me. I cannot believe I'm doing this." He whirled and stormed from the room.

Amber and I high-fived each either. We'd be much safer with a park ranger helping us.

Chapter Fourteen

Eric and I sat at the small table in my house and pulled up the security video over the last few days. The musky scent of his cologne and press of his shoulder against mine made it hard to concentrate.

"Is that Rose Flower?" Eric leaned closer.

Focus, CJ. "Obviously, she isn't following her mother's orders." I peered closer at the screen. "Wait. No, I don't think that's her, but it's definitely a woman." The tighter fitting hoodie revealed a woman's curves. My heart leaped. Could we have caught our thief on film? The figure slipped under the crime-scene tape and into the vacant house.

"What are you hiding in there?" Eric murmured. "Let's look at more footage to see what else she's been up to."

The woman appeared in and out of camera range, careful not to show her face. She stayed out of sight longer around the Olson house, but stepped back into the house, then headed toward the community entrance.

"Feel like going on a quest?" I closed the laptop and stood. "Maybe we'll see something we missed before."

We hurried to his side-by-side and sped to the last house in the community. "When are they going to take down the tape?" I ripped it away from the house.

"You shouldn't do that." Eric took the tape and let it flutter to the ground. "This is technically still a crime scene. It will be even more so when we show Davis the video footage." He handed me a pair of gloves.

"Oops." Not really. I was growing tired of the police department moving at a snail's pace. I pulled on the gloves, then pushed open the door and stood for a moment, taking in what I might have missed before. The house looked the same except for the absence of dust where Eric had fallen after being tased. This time we'd check every inch, even loose floorboards.

"I'll take the loft," Eric said, thundering up the stairs.

I started in the tiny freezer. I'd heard somewhere that people froze their valuables. Such was not the case this time. Other than an empty ice cube tray, the freezer/refrigerator was empty.

"Anything?" Eric called.

"No, you?"

"*Nada.*"

I pulled open the drawers under the stairs. Empty. I checked the tiny bathroom and came up with nothing. Stepping back, I pressed my lips together. The house was laid out exactly like the other rentals. There had to be something different I wasn't seeing, like the extra space under the floor in my house. From the sounds coming from upstairs, Eric wasn't having any luck either.

Hold on. The small kitchen seemed tinier. The pantry was gone, covered over with wood.

Smiling, I ran my hand over the wood paneling. Ah. My fingers slipped into a groove. Taking a firm grip, I slid the paneling aside to reveal shelves loaded with jewelry and electronics. Bingo. "Found it!"

Eric swung down from the loft. "Clever girl."

"Now what?"

"We call Davis and guard the treasure while we wait." He placed the call, then sat cross-legged on the floor.

I slid down the wall next to him. "That wasn't as hard as I'd thought. After the hidden floor in my house, I thought it might be something similar. It makes Lenora look suspicious, doesn't it?"

"I wonder whether any of the other tenants have hidden spaces. Is it a trend or only for the untrusting? The woman on the security footage didn't walk like Lenora. Could we be dealing with two people?"

No, Lenora walked with a limp, and Eric's question held merit. I wrapped my arms around them around my bent knees, resting my chin on top. "I don't think we're ever going to find out the thief's identity."

"We will." He put a consoling arm around my shoulder. "She'll mess up eventually."

"Who tore down the tape?" Davis asked, entering the house.

"I did." I pushed to my feet. "It's a deterrent to renters."

He stared at me as if I'd lost my mind, which I suppose I had. "I ought to reprimand you for crossing that tape, but since you found solid evidence, we'll let it slide…this time." He peered into the hidden cupboard. "Busy thief."

"I have a feeling the thief will move on now that we've found her hiding place." I frowned. "Is there any way of leaving it? Maybe she doesn't know we've been here. We can catch her when she comes back."

"That's a good idea, CJ." Davis grinned. "I'll have Milton and Perk keep an eye on the place. Your job here is done."

"What if she doesn't return?"

"Then we keep plodding along."

Leaving things in Davis's hands, Eric drove me home. After he left, I sat outside with a glass of iced tea and congratulated myself on almost catching the thief. If the police did nab her, it would be because of the work Eric and I had done. I wished I could join the stakeout later that night.

Who would it be? I ran down the list of female suspects. Linda Boyles? Marcy Wilson? Lucy Flower? I'd bet money that all three owned a black hoodie. Most people did. They probably also had black yoga pants.

I sipped my tea. It could be someone else entirely, but my guess was still on one of them. Tonight might reveal the culprit. Not only would they go to jail for theft, but for attempted murder and assault. Yep, whoever they caught would go away for a long time.

I sat up straighter as Tammy ran toward me. "What's wrong?"

"I went to the envelope where I keep your change, and the money left over from the last shopping I did for you is gone." Tears welled in her eyes.

"Where did you have it?" I set my tea glass on the table.

"In my car. I guess I forgot to lock the door, although that would be rare for me. I'm so sorry. I'll work off the money, I promise."

"Come on. I'll help you look." She'd gone shopping yesterday, which meant the thief had struck last night or early this morning.

When we arrived at her older model car, I noted where she'd parked in relation to the security cameras. Definitely in a blind spot. Which meant the thief knew about the cameras and only cared some of the time whether she'd be seen.

I leaned over and checked under the front seats and in between them. Not even a bread crumb. "You keep a clean car."

"I value cleanliness and order. That's why I'm confused as to how I left my door unlocked." Tammy thrust her hands into the pockets of her jeans.

"Maybe one of your family members got into the car?"

"Why would they? I went to bed later than they did because I was busy typing something for Mags.

Roy has an alarm on the door now to prevent Danny from sneaking out."

"Hmm." I studied the car. Definitely a conundrum. My gaze fell on the old-fashioned door locks. I closed the door. "Did you leave your window cracked open?"

"No."

"Where was the envelope?"

"Center console."

Right where anyone would see it. "I'm thinking someone jimmied your lock with a coat hanger or one of those things they stick between the door and the window."

"That's a lot of trouble for twenty dollars and some change." She peered closer at the window. "You're right. There's a scratch at the top of the window." She rubbed the spot with her finger.

"We'll have to report this. Maybe the police will be able to lift a fingerprint." I doubted it, but maybe we'd get lucky.

We didn't. Perk arrived after I called and announced the car wiped clean. "This thief's not a dummy."

"Unfortunately. Why do you think they kept those stolen items in the house instead of selling them?"

He shrugged. "Maybe they haven't found a buyer. There's only one pawn shop in town, and we're keeping an eye on it."

The proverbial lightbulb went on over my head. I had a list of the stolen items, photos on some, and ID numbers on others. I'd bet Caper's pink collar that the thief was trying to sell online. "Thanks." I rushed home and opened my laptop.

After an hour of searching online shops, I spotted a missing diamond ring. I hadn't seen it in the cupboard, but I was fairly certain the ring belonged to one of the previous campers. I called Eric on the radio and waited on the porch for him to arrive.

"I had a brainstorm," I said the moment he drove up. "The thief is selling online. I found a piece of missing jewelry."

"You're amazing." He followed me into the house and compared the photograph I had to the picture on my laptop. "Looks the same to me."

"Should we bid on it?"

"It's up to two hundred dollars, CJ. Let me contact Davis and see what he advises." He placed the call, then turned back to me. "He said to keep track of the bidding and note who purchases the ring. He's on his way."

By the time Davis arrived, the bid was up to three-hundred dollars. "Whew," he said. "Why would anyone wear something that expensive camping?"

"I think the guy proposed to her by the lake," I answered. "She was afraid to lose the ring, according to Mr. Robinson, so left it in her duffel bag inside the tent, thinking it would be safe wrapped in her underwear."

He shook his head. "Hard lesson to learn about keeping valuables." He wrote down the name of the seller. "I'll have our tech guy try to trace this name. I know I'm going to regret saying this, but keep up the good work." He clapped me on the shoulder and strolled from the house.

Eric watched him leave, then glanced at me. "You two got something going on?"

"No, why?" Was he jealous? Dare I hope so?

"No reason, except he seemed a bit chummy." He glanced back at the open door, then the laptop. "Let's see if we can find the other items being sold."

We located a necklace of Mags' and a camera that belonged to Amber. Selling online seemed like a slow way of making money to me, but safer than using the only pawnshop in town. I leaned back. "The thief seems to know every move we make. She knows where the cameras are located and that the pawn shop is under surveillance. It has to be one of the residents here."

"I agree. Everything we do needs to be done secretively. No open doors or windows and no talking outside." He gave a firm nod. "We'll back that thief into a corner by giving them no other choice but to face us."

"You sound fully onboard now." I grinned.

"Oh, I am, sweetheart. I most certainly am." He wiggled his finger between himself and me. "We're a team."

I couldn't think of anything I liked more. If I'd have known that a smile from Davis would make Eric react this way, I'd have tried to elicit one sooner.

Chapter Fifteen

"I guess I'll never see that camera again," Amber said. "Good thing I was diligent about downloading the pictures from my vacation right away."

"Jewelry is more important." Mags, recovered from her poisoning, scowled. "All I have will be yours one day, you know."

Amber patted her arm. "I am grateful, but don't go dying anytime soon."

"I have no control over that." A smile teased at her lips.

"I'm so glad the two of you are getting along," I said, closing my front door against eavesdroppers.

"Quite boring, actually." Mags's smile widened. "Now, what's our next step?"

"Aren't we going to wait for Eric?" Amber's eyes widened. "Didn't you say he's with us now?"

"Yes, but he isn't keen on the idea of laying a trap, and he said he'd be gone all day patrolling the furthest part of the national park." I set the notepad of suspects on the coffee table and sidled to the sofa. "We're pretty certain the thief is a resident of Heavenly Acres. The top suspects are Marcy Wilson, Lucy Flower or her daughter, Rose, and Linda Boyles. Any thoughts?"

"We go door-to-door with a petition," Mags suggested. "Then one of us distracts while the other searches."

"I like the petition thing, but these houses are too small to search unnoticed." I tapped the pencil against my teeth. It wasn't difficult to get the owner to agree to any purchases I needed, so what could we petition for? I asked the others.

"A fountain in the common area," Mags said.

"Playground equipment," Amber added.

"A new sign?" I suggested. All good ideas. "What if we ask which of these three the residents would prefer?"

"You've a good head on your shoulders, CJ." Mags nodded. "We can't all go knocking. Too suspicious."

"I've work, so the two of you go." Amber gave her grandmother a stern glance. "Don't eat or drink anything."

"We'll go after dinner," I said. "Everyone works during the day."

"Good. I'll take a nap so I'm chipper." Mags stood. "Put that notebook somewhere safe, like the freezer."

I gave her a jaunty salute and slid the pad into a baggie, then placed it under some frozen hamburger meat. After they left, I decided to take a slow drive through the community. The wheels of the cart crunched over the gravel path. Birds twittered from trees. The sun sparkled across the lake. Everything seemed as it should be, but evil lurked behind the beauty. Evil I intended to flush out.

No one stirred in any of the suspects' houses, and I couldn't see in any of the windows. Drat blinds that fit windows. My snooping would have to wait.

After a simple meal of a frozen microwave dinner, once the working residents had returned, I went to pick up Mags. She stepped out of her house in a pumpkin orange suit that looked like a throwback to the sixties. "I'm underdressed," I said, glancing at my denim capris and pink tee shirt.

"Yes, you are. We're on official business. Go change." Mags pursed her lips together, smearing lipstick that matched her suit.

"You need to fix your face." I steered the cart back toward home. Change into what? Taking care of Gammy hadn't left much time for nice clothes. I settled on a pair of white capris and a flowery blouse.

"Better," Mags said, "but you need some clothes fitting of your stature in the community. You're kind of like the mayor. Where's your clipboard?"

I groaned and dug in a drawer until I found a purple clipboard I'd kept for some reason. "Can we go now?" I attached a sheet of computer paper on the board, wrote down the three things we'd ask questions about, and grabbed an ink pen.

"Now, we're ready." Mags tottered back to the cart, wobbling a little on kitten-heeled shoes, and climbed back into the seat.

"Your feet are going to be killing you by the time we're finished." I drove toward number two.

"It's a small price to pay in order to be taken seriously. Uh-oh. The newlyweds are eating outside. You have to go inside to see anything."

"I'm aware of that." I climbed from the cart, taking the clipboard with me. I hoped they'd invite me inside. "Good evening."

"Hey." Mark smiled up at me. "What brings you out and about?" His gaze flicked to Mags. "Official business, I presume?"

Mags gave me an "I told you so" look.

"Yes, I've some funds to spend on improvement and thought I'd see what the residents preferred."

"Would you like some coffee?" Linda stood. "I've a fresh pot on."

"We'd love some." Mags motioned her head toward the house. "CJ will help."

"That isn't necessary." Linda stepped into the house and almost closed the door on my foot. "Oh, well, okay. Come on in. There isn't room for more than one in the kitchen."

"I'll help you carry." I smiled, noting what looked like a new television that took up most of one wall. "Wow, I bet you feel like you're right in the middle of a movie."

"Silly, isn't it," she said, "but we came into some money, and Mark has always wanted a big screen."

Interesting. I waited until she poured four mugs of coffee, then carried two out to the table. "Nice TV," I said.

"Thanks." Mark grinned. "Linda found some

uncashed checks from our wedding."

Mags wiggled her eyebrows at me. "Lucky."

"Seems odd to misplace them, only to find them now." I glanced at the clipboard.

"Why?" Linda frowned. "Are you doubting me?"

"No, of course not. Now for the questions." I met her glare. "Would you rather have a fountain, playground equipment, or a new sign?"

"It doesn't matter, does it, sweetheart?" Mark glanced at Linda.

"Not really."

"Pick one," Mags said. "We can't make an official decision unless everyone chooses."

"Fountain," they said in unison, returning a smile to Linda's face.

Cute. They thought alike. I stood, coffee untouched. After Mags' poisoning, I wasn't taking any chances. "Thank you. As always, please don't hesitate to let me know if there is anything you need."

Next stop, house number six. If it weren't for Mags' heels, I'd have walked. Instead, we climbed back in the cart, drove the short distance, then climbed back out. No one sat outside this time.

A little boy around the age of nine or ten answered the door. "Mom, it's people selling something."

"Tell them to go away."

"You heard her." He started to close the door.

I held it open. "It's CJ Turley." I stepped inside without waiting for an invitation. "I've something to ask you."

Five pairs of eyes stared at me from various spots around the house. How did they manage with so many people under one tiny roof?

Lucy peered down from the loft. "Be right there."

"She needs money if anyone does," Mags whispered. "Imagine feeding and clothing this brood."

I spotted a shopping bag from a high-end boutique. How could she afford to shop there?

Rose caught me peeking and used her foot, sporting an expensive, sparkly gym shoe, to shove the bag under the sofa. She glared at me, obviously still angry about the whole Danny thing.

Lucy joined us. "What's up?"

I went through the whole spiel of options. "Do you have a preference?"

Laughing, she said, "playground, of course. Anything to get these kids out of the house. Why do you think I visit Dave every night?"

"Why indeed," Mags muttered. "Thank you for your time. We've noted your choice." She practically shoved me out of the house.

"What in the world, Mags?" I glared at her once we were back in the cart.

"Did you notice the bright red Keurig on the counter? Or the new microwave?"

"No, I was staring at a bag from a boutique and the eighty-dollar shoes on Rose's feet."

"She's got money coming from somewhere, and I'm not buying the found checks Boyles claimed. We need to find out where this abundance is coming from."

"We will. Let's visit Marcy, then go over our discoveries." I stopped at number ten.

Marcy opened the door just enough to peer out. "Yes?"

"May we come in?" I gave my best smile. "We're taking a survey, and I need to make sure everything in the rental is up to par."

"Everything is fine. What survey?" She kept the door firmly in place.

Short of shoving her aside, I wouldn't get in this time. I gave her the three choices.

"I'm a renter. Why would I care where the money goes?" She narrowed her eyes.

Good point. "Just being courteous."

"Unlike some people," Mags said. "Are you a hoarder? Making drugs?"

"What?" Marcy's eyes widened.

"There had to be a reason you won't let us in."

"I wasn't expecting company, and I'm not dressed. You're a crazy old woman."

"So I've been told." Mags hooked her arm with mine and hurried us back to the cart. "You'll have to let yourself in tomorrow."

"I can't violate her privacy." I pulled free. "The tenant needs notice before I enter for any reason."

"That does us no good. If she's hiding something, she'll put it where we don't see it." She crossed her arms. "Where to now?"

"Let's visit Amber and see what she has to say about all this."

"Good job," Amber said, clapping. "We still have three solid suspects."

"I'd hoped to eliminate one or two." I plopped

onto her sofa. "Any idea how to find out how these people are affording nice things?"

"They all work and receive paychecks." She sat across from me, leaving the other end of the sofa to Mags. "Both of the Boyles work, Lucy works as well and probably gets social security after her husband's death. I'm not sure what Marcy does, but she leaves every day. You can't base your suspicions on them making purchases. The only surefire way of putting one of them at the top of the suspect list would be to see one of the stolen items in their house."

"We wasted our time." Mags sagged in her seat.

"Not necessarily." Amber laid a hand on her arm. "You know a little more about these people. Knowledge is power."

Unfortunately, not the power we needed at the moment. "If one of them is the thief, we need to make sure they know we're actively investigating. Maybe that will flush them out."

"How do you propose we do that?" Mags raised her eyebrows.

"I don't know yet, but I'll think of something." Maybe. Hopefully.

I drove Mags home, made sure she got inside safely, then parked the cart next to my house. Fetching Caper from inside, I clipped a leash on her collar and walked along the lake's shore. Not yet fully dark, there was plenty of light to see the path and I found myself stopping at the same spot Eric had once brought me. His thinking spot, he'd said. Maybe I'd find some clarity from the thoughts whirling around in my head.

I let Caper free to roam and settled my gaze on the water. Yes, all the suspects worked outside the home according to their contracts, but widows, teachers, and a receptionist didn't make that much money. Of course, it didn't cost a lot to live at Heavenly Acres either. Maybe I was looking in the wrong place for the thief.

We all agreed our culprit lived in the neighborhood, but I was too focused on their high-end purchases. I picked up a smooth stone and skipped it across the water. I needed to start asking different questions, ones that might reveal how much or how little they knew about the robberies.

Satisfied that I had a better plan, I called Caper to my side and reclipped her leash. I went home with a spring in my step until I spied a sheet of paper tacked to my front door. With my heart near my throat, I read, *Stop nosing around or suffer worse than Mags.*

Chapter Sixteen

"Look what I got." I flagged Eric down as he drove past my house the next morning.

He read the paper. A muscle ticked in his jaw. "Why do you sound thrilled to get a threat?"

I grinned. "Because this means one of the three people Mags and I visited last night is our thief."

"You went out without me?" His face darkened. "We talked about this, CJ." He thrust the paper at me. "Mags could have died and now you're getting death threats. When are you going to stop?"

"When the thief is caught."

"Hey, Ranger." Red Jones jogged toward us. Anger emanated from his body. "Someone stole my prize belt buckle. I won it in a rodeo a long time ago."

"Are you sure you didn't misplace it?" Why steal a belt buckle? It couldn't be sold, could it?

He slapped his gut. "It's always on my belt. This belt. Do you see it?"

I shook my head.

"Then it's gone. I had it before I went to bed last night. Always hang my belt on a hook by the door so I can put it on last thing before I leave for the day." He crossed his arms. "What are you two gonna do about it?"

"Did you call the police?" Eric leaned on his steering wheel.

"You're the ones in control around here."

"Hop in." Eric sighed. "We might as well take a look."

I climbed in beside Red and held on while Eric sped toward number twelve. I hadn't seen anything on the security video last night, but the thief kept out of sight of the cameras when doing the thieving.

Red's house was as sparsely furnished as Mags' was crowded. Next to the door hung a rusty coat hook. I didn't see any signs of a break-in.

"How would they have gotten your buckle?"

He hung his head. "I slept with the window open last night. I don't have much worth taking. Why would they want the silver buckle?"

"If it's sold, can they trace it back to you? Is there actually a market for a buckle?" I glanced from one man to the next. Our thief had seen an opportunity and taken it.

"It's the same buckle given to any winner." Red dropped onto a hard wooden chair. "Easy enough to say it once belonged to a famous rider, I suppose. If you don't look at the name and date engraved on the back." His shoulders sagged. "I'm too old to win another."

Eric clapped a hand on the man's shoulders. "We'll help you get it back." He motioned his head for me to follow him back outside. "I was going to suggest you have all the locks changed on the rentals, but keeping a window open is inviting the thief."

"I could send out a memo warning the residents about doing anything to make stealing easy." If we didn't wrap this up soon, word would get out, and I'd never rent the empty rentals.

"I'm sorry I got so upset about you going out last night." Eric climbed into his vehicle. "I understand why. It's only that…I worry about you." He settled a warm gaze on me. "I don't want anything to happen to you, Clarice Josephine."

I swallowed past the lump in my throat. "I'll be careful." I put a hand on his. "I've been a caregiver for such a long time I don't know how not to go to the aid of these people."

"You're a fix-it type of person." He gave a sad smile. "I'll do my best to keep you safe."

I leaned my head on his shoulder. "I know."

He turned the key in the ignition. "I'll take you home so you can work on that memo, and I'll call Davis. I've got him on speed dial." A chuckle vibrated his chest. "Not that I want another man around with his eye on you."

Heat rose up my neck and settled on my face. I muttered something about him having nothing to worry about.

"A guy always worries about other men when he's with a girl like you."

I jerked my eyes to his face, unsure whether he'd paid me a compliment or not. When he winked, I decided to bask in the feeling he might actually like me, and keep my questions to myself.

"I've doughnuts and coffee while we wait for Davis," I said. Eyeing the picnic table with longing, I led Eric into my house. Such a shame to waste good weather on the chance someone might be listening to our conversation. I'd seen all the suspects leave that morning and refused to be confined to my house out of fear. "Let's take this outside."

"I agree. It's a beautiful morning." Eric took the box of doughnuts from me while I made two cups of coffee.

When I joined him, he held a jelly-filled doughnut in his hand, but stared across the lake. "What is it?" I asked, following his gaze.

He leaped to his feet and sprinted for the water, dropping his doughnut in the grass. I set the mugs on the table and followed as Eric splashed into the water making a beeline for a partially submerged log.

"Help me." He waved me over.

I entered the water and helped him roll the log off of a body. "It's that camper whose girlfriend shot him." Dead eyes stared back at me, a bullet hole between them. "Do you think the girlfriend came back and finished the job?"

"Somebody did." Eric grabbed the body under the arms and dragged it to shore, dropping it at Davis's feet. Milton and Perk frowned behind him.

"Always something happening around here," the detective said.

"Especially when Miss Turley is around, it seems." Milton's frown deepened.

I glared in his direction, then ignored the man. "Things are hopping around our community."

"Murder and a stolen belt buckle." Davis squatted next to the body. "Looks like we found the belt buckle." He pointed to something silver peeking out of the man's pocket.

"That means whoever shot him is our thief." I glanced from Eric to Davis. "Why give him the buckle, then kill him?"

Eric shrugged. "Maybe he wasn't keen on receiving stolen goods as a gift and threatened to tell the authorities."

"Maybe." Davis pushed to his feet. "Officer Perk, case the scene. Milton, you come with me to visit Mr. Jones. Miss Turley, while I appreciate the vision you make, you might want to change your clothes."

I glanced down, registering the fact that I wore a white tee shirt, fully transparent from the lake water. I shot a wide-eyed glance at Eric's grin, then dashed for the house and up the stairs. This had to be the most embarrassing thing I'd ever done. I know Eric had been busy pulling a dead body from the lake, but a warning would have been nice. Grams would roll over in her grave at the spectacle I'd made of myself.

"CJ?" Eric knocked on the open front door.

"Be right down." I finished changing and joined him in the living space. I crossed my arms. "You should have said something."

"I didn't notice until Davis mentioned it."

"Oh?" I took a step back. How should I take the fact he hadn't noticed I wore little more than my bra?

"I was busy." He tilted his head and grinned. "But once Davis mentioned it—"

"Oh, shut up." I marched outside to retrieve the mugs of cold coffee and throw away the doughnuts.

"Hey, I wasn't finished." Eric reached for the box.

I held it behind me. "Do you really want to chance eating something left out and unguarded after what happened to Mags?"

"Good point." He paled. "Got any eggs? I could make us an omelet."

I shuddered. "I don't have an appetite after...that," I said, thinking of the body.

"All right, want to take a ride? I thought I'd head over to the victim's campsite and look around before the police arrive and block it off."

I grinned, tossing the box of doughnuts into the garbage. "That's a great idea." I left the mugs on the table and climbed into his side-by-side. "We'd better hurry. I don't know how much time we'll have."

"Not long enough, I guarantee it." He sped around the lake, me holding onto the dashboard for dear life, and skid to a halt in front of the victim's tent. He handed me a pair of gloves.

"You're always prepared."

"I was a Boy Scout." He jumped from the vehicle and ducked through the tent flap.

I followed at a much slower pace. A robbery crime scene and a murder crime scene could be two different things. I peeked inside, relieved to see no blood. "He wasn't killed here."

"No, he wasn't. Since I didn't hear a gunshot last night, I'm willing to bet his murderer used a silencer."

"That sounds experienced. Do you think his killer and the thief are the same person, because that's scary." Until Mags got poisoned, I'd thought our thief was just someone desperate for money. If our thief killed this man, they weren't messing around.

Eric took me by the arm. "Let's pay a visit to Robinson. Maybe he heard something or someone told him they did."

"Where would the victim have been killed? Close to the water? Ronnie Ward wouldn't have been easy to carry." I jogged to keep up with his fast pace.

"We'll look there after paying Robinson a visit." He faced me. "A gunshot like that, the man would have died instantly. He wasn't killed in the tent."

I shuddered. "We need to find out where he was shot."

"Yes." He didn't speak again until we reached Robinson's trailer. "We've got to be careful."

"I thought Robinson was safe." My blood chilled.

"I don't trust anyone at this point." He slipped out of the vehicle and held out his hand to me.

I slid mine into his larger one and let him lead me to the man sitting in a lawn chair. Eric's protectiveness filled me with emotions I didn't know how to process. One minute he scolded me out of fear for my safety, the next he treated me as something precious and worthy of saving.

"Morning, Ranger." Robinson blew a plume of cigar smoke into the air.

"A man was shot and killed last night. Did you hear anything?"

Robinson's eyes widened, and he snuffed his cigar out on the sole of his work boot. "Not a thing, and no other camper has complained. Which site?"

"Ronnie Ward. Twenty-one."

"Are you sure?" his brow furrowed. "He was supposed to check out today."

"Looks like he checked out early." I gave a nervous giggle, then pressed my lips together as both men stared at me.

Eric gave a subtle shake of his head, then returned his attention to Robinson. "We're still having things go missing from the tiny houses. The police have launched a full investigation."

"I'll keep my eyes and ears open. By the way, those cleaning supplies showed up a couple of days ago right here next to the trailer. Guess the stranger isn't going to clean the bathrooms anymore."

"No need to pretend to be anything but what she is," I said. "A thief with no respect for other people."

"How do you know it's a woman?" Robinson asked.

"We've seen her on camera. Thanks for the help, man." Eric thrust out his hand. "You should have told us about the cleaning supplies the minute they showed up."

"I've been gone on a fishing trip for a couple of days." Robinson shook his hand. "They were here when I got back."

"Who runs the campsite when you're gone?" I asked.

"I hire a company to watch things when I'm gone. Campground Babysitters, Inc. They stop by a couple of times a day to check on things." He pulled a folded piece of paper from his pocket. "Here's their phone number, no address, and I've never met them. I post the phone number on the website in case someone wants to book a site or check out."

Eric took the paper. "Thanks. We'll check them out." Once we were back in the side-by-side, he said, "What if someone from this company babysat the campground one day and saw what easy pickings the tiny homes were?"

Chapter Seventeen

"Call the number. We can say we're looking into using them for my future vacation."

"You're taking a vacation?" He arched an eyebrow.

"No, but they don't know that." I rocked on the balls of my feet. "I'll call." I grabbed the paper and punched the numbers into my phone. After the third ring, a woman answered.

"Campground Babysitters."

"Yes, do you babysit mobile home parks or tiny house communities?"

The woman didn't speak, but I could hear her breathing on the other end. "Why?"

"Uh." I hadn't expected to be questioned. "I'm going on vacation?"

"I suppose I could fill in for you."

"What's the address to your business so we can meet to discuss details? My name is CJ Turley, and I—" Click. I frowned. "She hung up on me."

"Why?"

"You heard what I said. As soon as I mentioned my name…oh." I'd just spoken to the thief. "We need to give this number to Davis right away."

"Did the voice sound familiar?" Eric put his hands on my shoulders and peered into my eyes. "Would you recognize the person if you spoke with them again?"

"I don't know. Maybe. She had an ordinary voice." I could barely remember names, much less voices. If I didn't associate my tenants with their house number, I'd be completely lost.

"Let's go." Eric grabbed my hand and we rushed back to the victim's tent where Davis and Milton searched the area. Eric explained about the phone number and how they'd hung up when I said my name.

"Good work." Davis pocketed the paper. "Time to step down, Mr. Drake. Things are getting too dangerous and you don't have the authority to pursue the investigation."

Eric squared his shoulders. "I do have some authority. This is my park."

That's how I felt about Heavenly Acres, of course I had no training, just a desire to do well by my tenants. We were getting close to stopping the thief—I felt it in every part of me. If I were to stop snooping, the crook wouldn't know I had. They'd still threaten and watch me, so why not see this through?

"What are you thinking, Miss Turley?" Davis narrowed his eyes.

"Short of arresting me, you cannot keep me from trying to stop the person threatening me and my friends." I slipped my arm through Eric's and headed for the side-by-side.

"Do not test my patience," Davis called.

I waved a dismissive hand and climbed into my seat. "Let's investigate the lake shore."

Eric smiled and shook his head. "I don't know whether you're brave or foolish, but I think I like this side of you."

"I'm probably a bit of both." I returned his smile and glanced at a stony-faced Davis. We'd have to be more careful about what we did or we would end up behind bars.

Eric inched along the shore as we studied the ground around us, searching for where Ward had been shot. It felt like looking for that elusive needle in knee high grass.

Eric stopped so suddenly my head whipped forward. "Sorry." He jumped out and knelt in a spot of trampled underbrush. "I've found blood."

"I'll stay in my seat, thank you."

Laughing, he stood and turned in a slow circle. "I wonder if she ditched the murder weapon."

"Why? We'd find it. At least they always do in the movies and it's a key step to locating the killer." I propped my feet on the dashboard. "With today's technology, they can find out almost anything if they have the murder weapon."

"You watch too much television."

I shrugged. "I enjoy my crime drama shows. It can't all be fiction." When he moved away, I sat up, my feet falling to the floorboard. "Where are you going?"

"I'm following some tracks. Bring your phone

and snap a picture. I want to compare it to the muddy prints you found in Mags' house."

Right. Boy Scout and park ranger. He had to know a few tricks in regard to tracking people. I hopped to the ground and followed, taking pictures when he told me to.

The shooter had run through brush in desperate need of being cleared, but since we lived in The Natural State, things stayed the way they grew until deemed necessary to cut down. The trail led around and back to the church.

I stopped and marveled at the sun's rays through the tree branches glinting off the new windows. If someone were to deface any part of this peaceful building, I'd personally throttle them. "Did she go inside?"

"Doesn't look that way, but she did head for the community."

Which meant we lost her trail on the gravel drive. "Hold on. I think I've seen this tread before. Does it belong to Converse?"

Eric whipped around. "I was thinking Nike, but it shouldn't be too hard to find out. Let's head to town and visit a shoe store."

An hour later we matched the print to a shoe by the trade name, Vans. I also knew where I'd seen a shoe like the new one in my hand. "We need to ask Rose Flower a few more questions, and before you say anything, we are not telling Davis of our discovery until *after* we've spoken to the girl."

Eric grinned. "As long as we do tell him, I don't have a problem waiting an hour."

"The man's extremely busy," I said smiling.

"We're doing him a favor by not adding to his work load until we have something to tell him."

"That's my girl."

A smile remained on my face all the way to the Flower house.

"You've got to stop harassing my daughter." Lucy peered through a slightly open door. "Do you know how many people in the world wear Vans? Especially teenagers? Do you really think my Rose is capable of murder?"

I narrowed my eyes. "How did you know there was a murder?"

"Everyone knows that someone tried to poison Mags. It isn't as if she's kept the fact a secret."

Oops, I almost let loose something vital to the investigation. I cut a chagrined glance at Eric.

He rolled his eyes. "We're just checking all avenues, Lucy."

She exhaled slowly. "I'll fetch my daughter." A few minutes later, she stepped outside with a sullen Rose. "Tell them."

Tears sprang in the girl's eyes. "Someone stole my Vans. I set them on the porch yesterday to dry after I cleaned them."

Eric shared a glance with me. "We need to find a woman with the same size feet as Rose."

"That doesn't explain the prints inside Mags' house."

"Wait for it," Lucy said.

We all stared at Rose.

She sighed. "I stole the shoes out of a car at the campgrounds." She jerked her head up. "That's all I've stolen, I swear. I wanted those shoes so bad."

I couldn't help but laugh. "You stole the thief's shoes, then she stole them back. You can't make this stuff up." Stranger than fiction, but why take back the shoes? By leaving them in Rose's possession, suspicion would have been on the girl. There was something Rose wasn't telling us. "What are you holding back?"

"Fine." Her tears spilled down her cheeks. "I did steal the shoes, and they must have seen me. I got a note a few days later with twenty dollars and a threat they'd call the police and report the theft unless I—"

"Unless you what?"

"Unless I agreed to case the community at night for open or unlocked houses. They're my prints inside Mags' house."

"That still doesn't explain why they took the shoes back."

Eric stared across the lake for a moment. "Was there anything strange about the shoes?"

"Like what?" Rose wiped her tears on the sleeve of her shirt.

"You tell me."

She shook her head. "I loved those shoes. They had sparkles along the seams. I've never seen them in a store before."

Sparkles? "Diamonds." I grinned. "That's why she wanted the shoes back. She glued stolen diamonds on them until she could find a buyer." Mags had a missing tennis bracelet that could have been torn apart. Personally, I would have buried the diamonds, but to each his own.

"I had diamonds on my feet?" Rose's eyes

widened and she sagged against her mother.

"Possibly. Thanks for clearing things up." I headed back to the vehicle with Eric. "Now what?" I asked, sliding into my seat.

"We need to find those shoes. The question is how?"

"We're back to laying a trap."

"Nope." He turned the vehicle around and drove back to my house. "Let's start with making stealing harder. Finish the fliers and distribute them yourself. That way we know they actually reached the residents."

"It's a plan." I flashed him a grin and darted into my house. An hour later, I started the door-to-door hike.

"Hey, Mags." I smiled and held out a flier.

She took it, frowning. "How is this going to help us catch the thief? It's going to make it harder."

"I know, but Eric is insistent that we not lay a trap. Maybe the thief will get frustrated and make a mistake." One could always hope. "Want to walk with me?"

"Not tonight. Someone needs to spend time in deep thought to solve this case." She sighed. "I guess it will have to be me."

"Okay, let me know if you come up with something." I chuckled and continued on my way, Caper bounding at my heels and sending bugs scurrying from bushes. "I wish you were a hound dog. Then we could have you sniff out this elusive thief." I got a tail wag.

With a wine glass in hand, Lucy scowled from

the steps of Dave Lincoln's house. I didn't blame her with all the times I'd accused her daughter of something. At least I could deliver two fliers at once. "Good evening. We're asking y'all to be proactive in stopping the thefts." I handed them each a flier.

"I thought the cameras would deter the thief," Dave said. "I've valuables in my house, precious memorabilia. If you can't keep them safe, I may have to move on."

"We're doing our best, sir. My suggestion to you is to keep them locked up in something that can't be broken into." I'd hate to lose a tenant, but I understood his concern. "The police and park ranger are actively trying to close this case."

"What about Mags' attempted murder? Is it connected?"

"I can't say. That would be up to the authorities." I shot Lucy a frown. She'd been talking too much.

The woman didn't seem the least bit affected by my frown. Too many of her own "Mom" looks to her brood of children, I supposed. "We shouldn't be talking about this until the killer is caught."

"If there's a killer on the loose, we should be made aware," Lucy said. "I've children to protect."

As she left them home under the care of a thirteen-year-old. I bit my tongue to keep from saying what I wanted, excused myself, and continued delivering the fliers until I'd made the circle and arrived home. The remaining fliers could be distributed at the campground tomorrow.

"Good grief."

Held in place with a knife through my front door was one of the fliers with a big X through it.

Chapter Eighteen

"Without a doubt, the thief is one of the residents," I said when Eric arrived after my radio call.

"This is getting serious." He lowered his tall frame to my sofa. "Last time they used tape, this time a knife. Did you call Davis?"

"Right after I radioed you." I sat next to him, my heart racing. I had to admit to a trickle of fear now. For the first time, I realized I had allowed myself to get too deep into the case. There was absolutely no turning back now. Despite the fear, I didn't want to turn back. For the first time in my life, I was doing something that thrilled me. Something exciting, but did I want to die catching a thief?

A knock sounded at the door. Eric told me to remain seated and answered, one hand on the gun on his hip. It seemed he never went anywhere without it lately. "Come in, Davis."

The detective immediately took a stance in front

of me. "Is there someone you can stay with, CJ? A murder and a threat with a knife is nothing to take lightly."

"Nope, I'm all alone in the world."

"No, you aren't." Eric sat back next to me and took my hand in his. "You have me, Amber, and Mags. I can stay here with you and sleep on the sofa."

A short laugh escaped me at the thought of him curling up on my loveseat. "If I choose that option, I'll take the love seat." I stood and paced the small area not filled with two large, muscular men who took up a lot of space. "Mags' house is too crowded already, and her cat doesn't like my dog. Amber might be a possibility, but..." I faced them. "This is my home. The only one I've ever had of my own. I don't want to leave it."

"Then I'm staying." Eric set his jaw. "It's only temporary."

"Really?" I tilted my head. "How close are we to catching this person?"

"Closer than yesterday." Davis dropped the knife into a bag. "Maybe there will be fingerprints on this."

"There won't." I fetched my laptop and set it on the coffee table, then pulled up the night's video footage. Clear as day the hooded thief/murderer tacked the flier on my door. "What's the name of Ronnie Ward's killer? I deserve to know at this point."

"Addie Morris, no prior record." Davis's eyes hardened. "You are not to tell a single person that name. She is our prime suspect."

"If you can find her." I crossed my arms. "I'm sure you've visited her last known address."

He nodded. "Neighbors haven't seen her in a month. She told them she was taking an extended vacation. She's in business for herself, but no one knows what exactly she does."

"Campground Babysitter."

"No address for them either, just the phone number that belongs to a burner phone."

"So we know a whole lot that goes nowhere," I said, slumping against the loveseat's throw pillows.

"We have a name. That's something." Davis stared at me for a minute. "We'll be doing a more intensive study of your residents. One of them is a killer."

"I determined that for myself, thank you." And planned on speaking with Lenora again at the first opportunity. The woman had to know more than she let on. After all, she'd been the overseer for a longer period of time than I had.

"Don't do anything without running it past me," Davis said. "I'm serious. I'll lock you up for your own protection if I have to."

"Duly noted." I'd take the chance. "Eric will be a sufficient guard dog, Detective."

He didn't look convinced but left us anyway.

"I'll get a blanket. You take the bed. Sorry, I can't offer you clean sheets." I stood, only to find myself stopped by Eric grabbing my hand.

He tugged me close and cupped my face, peering deeply into my eyes. "What is it, sweetheart?"

My chin quivered. "I honestly don't know. Only

that I've always taken care of someone, my parents, Grams, and now that I'm on my own, wanting to take care of my residents...well, a simple thief has turned into a killer, and I'm in the crosshairs."

"So stop," his voice lowered, and his eyes grew dreamy.

"I don't want to." I was drowning. If he asked me again to stop, I would.

"Then I'll do my best to help the prettiest girl in Arkansas catch this killer. I'm going to kiss you now, Clarice Josephine."

My name sounded beautiful coming from his lips. I closed my eyes as his head lowered.

Something crashed through my front window.

Caper yelped and ducked under the loveseat.

We jerked apart, Eric thrusting me behind him.

A rock wrapped with another flier had prevented me from having my first ever real kiss. I wanted to bash whoever threw it in the head.

Eric unwrapped the rock and read, "You might want to get another job and move on while you can." He raised his gaze to meet mine. "Two threats in one night isn't good."

"What I'd like to know is how that person got two fliers when I put one directly into every resident's hand." Either Lucy or Dave had to have tossed theirs. It was the only explanation. "As for their message, forget it. I like my job and my house, and I'm not going anywhere."

I marched up the stairs to fetch a blanket. When I came back down, I waved a dismissive hand at Eric and lay down. "Go to bed. This will all still be here in the morning."

He looked at me as if I'd gone nuts. "I can't leave you down here alone after that."

"Well, I'm not leaving."

"Fine, I'll bed down on the floor, what there is of it." He took the stairs two at a time, returning with every blanket and pillow from my bed. With short, angry movements, he made a pallet between me and the coffee table, pounded the pillows to the shape he wanted, and prepared to go to sleep.

"Stubborn man."

"Stubborn woman."

I smiled and closed my eyes, feeling warm and safe.

When I woke, Eric stood at my kitchen counter making coffee. He glanced over and smiled. "You snore."

"I do not." I stood and stretched. "How did you sleep?"

"Not bad, considering. You?"

"Not as comfortable as my bed, but okay." I accepted the offered coffee. "I plan on speaking to Lucy first thing. It's Saturday, so she'll be home if I get there early enough."

"Why?"

"I want to know what she did with her flier."

"We'll have to make it fast. Davis will be here soon to take the rock, and I want to get your window fixed."

"Roy can do that. It's his job. I was going to deliver fliers to the campground. After last night, do you think it's worth it? We know the killer is one of ours."

"I do think it beneficial to let them be on their

guard against theft. Robinson won't like it because it might hurt his business."

"All the more reason to catch this person. Summer camping season is fast approaching." Robinson wouldn't be the only one losing money. I wouldn't be able to fill the rest of my rentals at this rate. I might lose the very job I wanted to keep.

After Roy arrived, and I told him to put my window at the top of his day's priority list, Eric escorted me to Lucy's house. Sleepy-eyed and in pajama pants and a tank top, she sat on her stoop nursing a cup of coffee.

"You again? You're like a tick burrowing under my skin," she said.

"Sorry. One question, please."

"Really?" She gave me a sarcastic tilt of her head. "Only one?"

"What did you do with the flier I gave you last night?"

"I threw it away. I didn't want to bring it home and scare my kids. Why?"

"No reason. Thanks." I climbed back into the side-by-side with Eric. "As I thought, she tossed her flier, making it easy for the killer to get her hands on a second one."

"Great because Davis just pulled up in front of your place." We circled back to my house and told Davis about the rock.

Roy already worked at replacing the window. "You want Danny to come stay with you, CJ? He might be of some use."

"No, thank you. Eric is here."

He narrowed his eyes. "People won't be talking

if it's Danny."

Eric turned to hide his smile.

Davis's eyes flashed. "Mr. Drake is more qualified to keep someone out of harm's way. Plus, he's licensed to carry a gun. If people want to talk, let them, or better yet, tell them it's my order for this man to stay."

"Makes no difference to me." Roy shrugged. "I just thought she might want to protect her reputation."

"I'd rather protect my life." I smiled. "But I do appreciate your thoughts. It's best if Danny stay safe at home."

Davis took the rock and second flier, then motioned for us to join him next to his car. "Too many people know too much about this case. That's why it's so hard for us to catch this woman. CJ, you're asking too many questions, and it's impeding my investigation."

I crossed my arms. "Do you have a problem with my handing out fliers at the campground?"

"Can you do it without spewing details?"

"Of course."

"Hmmph." He climbed into his car. "Eric, you've got your hands full, that's for sure." He slammed the door and sped away.

Eric took my hand. "I like what my hands are full of." He flashed me a grin. "Ready to distribute the rest of those fliers?"

Face flaming, I nodded, wishing for another opportunity for the kiss we'd almost shared last night. Instead, I climbed into his vehicle, resolving to be content with Eric's company.

We parked in front of Robinson's trailer. He stepped outside to greet us. "I've seen more of you, Ranger, in the last few days than ever."

"Hopefully, we won't have this type of circumstance again. We'd like to hand out fliers warning the campers to lock up their valuables."

Robinson's expression turned grave. "Word will get around and ruin business. That yellow crime scene tape is bad enough."

"Are you saying we can't?" I asked.

"Not exactly. How's business on your side of the lake?"

"No one has left."

"No new renters either, I bet."

"No new." My shoulders slumped. "We really need to catch this person, Mr. Robinson. That's the only way to return to normal."

"I ain't seen or heard a thing. Do you always bring trouble with you, young lady?"

"Nope, first time. Can we hand out the fliers or not?"

"No, but you can tack one to the board at the entrance. It's up to the campers to keep notified of what's going on."

It would have to do. Eric thanked the man and drove me to the entrance of the campgrounds. "Sorry, CJ."

"Better than nothing." I took one of the fliers and hung it next to an advertisement for camping gear. Right next to that was a simple page for House Babysitter. I smiled recognizing that phone number. Our thief had moved from watching campgrounds to watching houses, and I'd bet my favorite sneakers she did it to case the joints. I yanked the paper off the board and handed it to Eric. "I think we need a house sitter, don't you?"

"For whose house?"

"My Grams'."

Chapter Nineteen

Since I'd not had the heart to sell Gammy's house after she died, all it needed was a dusting. All of Grams' possessions, except Caper, of course, were still in place. I removed any sign of me and stepped back to see if I'd forgotten anything.

"Do you see anything that will tip off the babysitter that this house belongs to me or a relative of mine?"

Eric shook his head. "Why don't you live here? It's a cute house. Must be over a hundred years old, and someone spent money on renovations."

"Maybe someday. Right now, it's too big for just me and the dog. I like living on the lake." And having a real job. While caring for Grams, I rarely left this house except for doctor appointments. I wasn't ready to reside within its walls anytime soon. "Let's place the cameras and wait."

Eric placed the small white squares in strategic locations throughout the house, then we hurried to a rented car to slouch down, watch the screen of my phone, and wait. The cameras were motion-activated so even if we got distracted, we'd be alerted by anyone entering the house.

I slid down in my seat and grinned at Eric. "This is fun."

He gave me a slow, sexy smile. "If it was dark, I'd give you that kiss we were interrupted on."

Mercy. My heart stopped. I couldn't breathe. Why not kiss me now? My eyes started to close in preparation.

"There's a car." Eric straightened.

Maybe we weren't supposed to have that kiss. I sighed and turned as a forest-green sedan pulled into the driveway. "That's a rental license plate."

"Sure is. She's going in the house."

Keeping her head down, the dark-haired woman fished the house key out of a porcelain frog's mouth, unlocked the door, and went inside. My phone buzzed immediately, and I pulled up the screen. "She's wearing one of those clear plastic masks with the lips and eyes painted on." Would we ever catch a break?

"She's a smart one, but they all mess up eventually."

The woman stood in the middle of the living room, obviously casing the place. Good luck. I'd stored everything of value. Unless she wanted an old television or microwave, she was out of luck.

She strolled into the kitchen as if she were going to bake a cake. The audacity.

"Darn it." I watched as she pocketed an antique scale. "I forgot about that."

"She won't leave the house with it, I promise."

Eric put a hand over mine. "As she heads for the door, put the speaker on. She'll drop everything she's taken."

"And run."

"Better than her taking your grandmother's things."

True, but I wanted to catch this woman so bad. She had several things to answer for, and Ronnie Ward deserved justice. "She doesn't look like a killer, does she?"

"Most of the time, they don't." Keeping his eye on the screen, he shifted in his seat. "I've helped capture some ordinary-looking people who thought they could hide in a national park. They'd get away with it for a while, but eventually someone would see them, and we'd make an arrest. It'll happen with this woman too."

"I'm learning that I am not a patient person."

He laughed. "It's a good thing you aren't a police officer. You'd hate stakeouts."

"Yeah, the whole gun thing, remember?" The woman started opening cabinets, even the freezer. I guess my hiding place at home wasn't such a good idea. All the thief would find in Grams' freezer was a credit card I'd already canceled and hadn't taken the time to thaw and toss.

She pulled the card out, turned it over, then returned it to its frozen resting place, no doubt noticing the expiration date. I really should turn off the electricity to Gammy's house, but having things on and food in the fridge helped the façade that someone lived there.

Not finding anything else, she moved to the

bathroom, then the guest bedrooms, finally stopping in the last room with a camera...Grams' room. Tears filled my eyes as the woman rummaged through my grandmother's things as if she were shopping at a flea market. I fought the urge to scream at her to stop.

She pocketed some cheap, but well-constructed costume jewelry that looked expensive but was actually worth little. After rifling through the closet, she headed for the front door.

I pressed the speaker button.

"Drop the items," Eric said, his voice booming into the house.

The woman froze and spun. When Eric spoke again, she emptied her pockets, then darted out the front door, leaving it open. She jumped into her car and sped from the driveway.

"Follow her." I clicked my seatbelt into place.

"Hold on. I'll do my best not to lose her." Eric pressed the accelerator, squealing tires.

We were close enough to the other car's rear bumper we could see the woman glance in her rearview mirror before increasing her speed. I held on for dear life and prayed no pedestrians would walk out in front of either of us. I didn't breathe again until we reached the freeway.

The suspect rocketed down the on-ramp and into traffic. Horns blared as we cut a car off in our pursuit. A younger driver raised his hand in an obscene gesture. I waved and mouthed, "sorry" as we continued the chase.

"What if we pass a police officer?" I asked.

"We'll deal with that when and if it happens.

Call Davis and tell him we're in pursuit. See if he can't get someone to cut this woman off before she causes an accident."

I did as I was told. "We're in pursuit of a woman who we caught trying to steal from my grandmother's house. We need someone to cut her off. We're on I-40 headed toward Little Rock. Suspect is driving a dark green Camry and wearing a mask."

"I know I'm not going to like the story behind this. I need to know what mile marker."

"We just passed 101."

"Sending a patrol car." Click.

"You sounded quite official," Eric said, grinning.

"Are you actually having fun?"

"Yep. When I was a kid, I wanted to be a NASCAR driver." He swerved around a truck. A horn blared as the other driver swerved. "This is as close as I'll get."

"Watch out." I clutched the handle over my head. "You came very close to that semi."

"Not even. Wow, that woman is a good driver." He increased our speed.

"I cannot believe you're impressed with her. She's killed people." My heart beat in my throat.

"Doesn't make her a bad driver." He hit the brakes, swerved around a vehicle pulling a trailer, and sped up again. "She's pulling ahead of us. Where is our backup?"

I glanced in the side mirror, spotting approaching whirling lights. "Police car coming up fast behind us."

"I was having fun, but it's best to leave this to the experts." He slowed and pulled into the left lane, letting the police take over. "We'll follow, but stay back a bit to be safe."

"Thank God." I released the tension in my shoulders. I realized something else that day— besides my lack of patience, I was also a big scaredy-cat and didn't like racing down the freeway.

Rather than kiss the bumper of the squad car as he'd tried to do with the thief, Eric kept one or two cars between us and the police, speeding up if they got too far ahead, then slowing, still surpassing the speed limit enough to keep me on edge.

The thief took a sharp turn over one of those paths that read, *Authorized Vehicles Only* and sped in the opposite direction. Both the police car and we passed by too fast to make the turn.

Eric slammed his hand against the steering wheel. "We came so close to catching her."

Disappointment surged through me. "It wasn't for lack of trying."

He veered toward the next exit and turned around to head for home. "All of our suspects have dark hair. That's all we learned today."

I forced a smile. "I learned that you like to drive fast and would have made a good race car driver."

"Thanks." He patted my hand. "You're a good sport."

Really? I'd never been called that before and always thought it was something one guy said to another after winning a game. Probably one of the least romantic things he could have said to me.

"Didn't you experience a thrill of the chase at all?"

Now that the threat of dying in a fiery car crash didn't loom in my near future, I paused to think. The adrenaline rush, the sweeping fear, the hope of catching the thief all combined to form an unforgettable experience. To share it with Eric was the cherry on top. I smiled. "I actually did, now that I think about it, but that doesn't mean I'm willing to repeat the experience."

He laughed, reaching for my hand and giving it a squeeze. "I really like you, CJ Turley. You're a riot."

I was pathetic enough to take any compliment I could get. "You aren't so bad yourself."

Davis waited in front of my house. "Your dog is barking."

"That's because you're out here." I opened the door and let Caper out. She sniffed the detective's shoes, then started digging under the house.

"It's unfortunate we lost the suspect," Davis said, sitting at my picnic table. "We'll try to pick up her trail by questioning the rental car company."

"I doubt she used her real name," Eric said. "I'm also guessing the housesitting business is as phony as the campground one."

"Now that's where you lost me." Davis crossed his arms. "I thought the two of you weren't going to do anything without running it past me first."

"Well," I sat at the table next to Eric. "We tacked a flier warning people about the thief on the campground board. That's when I spotted an advertisement for housesitting and recognized the phone number as the same one used for Campground Babysitting. We called, set up my grandmother's house, and prevented the thief from taking off with my grandmother's things." I met his stern gaze. "We had no idea she'd get away. It seemed like a foolproof plan."

"I thought you two were smart." He leaned his elbows on the table. "You could have died today." He held up a hand to stop Eric's protest. "Your idea of hiring a supposed house sitter was a good one. You messed up by not letting us handle the situation. We could have had someone waiting to grab her the moment she stepped outside."

"Are you saying it's our fault she got away?" I couldn't believe him. I stood. "We've done more in this investigation than the precinct's Laurel and Hardy. Even you, if I'm to be brutally honest."

His eyes narrowed. "Are you accusing me of being incompetent at my job?"

"Are you accusing me of negligently letting a thief get away?" I crossed my arms.

"All right, you two." Although Eric's eyes sparkled with what I had learned was the first stages of anger, he stepped between us. "We're all working together to catch this woman. There's no need to fight amongst ourselves."

I glared. "Doesn't it upset you for Davis to act this way toward us?"

"Sure, it does, but he's the authority here." He turned away from Davis and mouthed, "work with me here."

Oh. "Fine." I plopped back on the seat, more than willing to follow Eric's lead.

Davis held his thumb and forefinger a hair apart. "You are this close to going to jail."

I curled my lip. "I'll take my chances."

Eric gave me an exasperated look.

"Sorry."

Caper started yapping as a car drove slowly by us. Marcy Wilson, her head cocked in our direction, rolled by in a blue sedan, window down. Her head craned to watch us until she'd moved too far ahead.

"Suspect number one," I said.

Davis narrowed his eyes in my direction. "Why do you say that?"

"She wouldn't let me in her house when I was delivering fliers."

"So?" He smirked. "She values her privacy."

I cannot believe I thought the man attractive. "In my book, that means she's hiding something."

He pushed to his feet. "Leave people alone and let us handle this."

I wanted to tell him he sounded like a broken record, but the warning look on Eric's face stilled my tongue. Caper ran over and dropped something in my lap. I held up a gold chain.

Chapter Twenty

The three of us darted toward the house and fell on our knees. Different styles of jewelry sparkled from the hole my dog had dug.

"I had no idea this stuff was here." I sprang to my feet, taking a step back at the thunderous expression on Davis's face and the questioning one on Eric's. "You can't possibly think I put the jewelry under my house."

"To pretend to be investigating thefts would be the perfect cover-up." Davis crossed his arms.

"I guarantee you I'd be smarter than to leave things where my dog would find them." I could not believe he accused me of being the thief and covering my tracks in such a bizarre way. "I've spent hours—hours trying to catch the thief. Why waste my time like that? Besides, this started before I became the overseer."

"You could have gotten the job to help cover your tracks."

"What about the cameras?" I raised my

eyebrows.

"Film. You could be showing them to us as another ruse. Crooks will often resort to extraordinary means not to be captured."

"You can leave now." I slumped back on the picnic table bench. "Both of you." My heart felt ripped to shreds at the lack of support Eric gave me. Maybe I would quit this job I loved so much and become a recluse at Grams'. It was better than having to see the man I was falling for look at me with distrust.

"I'm not going anywhere," Davis said. "At least not until Milton and Perk get here."

"You're turning my house into a crime scene?" My heart dropped further.

"We are going to search the house, yes." He unclipped the radio on his belt and stepped off to the side to place a call.

"You can still go." I glared at Eric.

"No, I won't." He sat next to me. "I know you aren't the thief, CJ. I'm sure Davis does too. He's not a stupid man."

"The thief put those things under my house for this very reason." Relief that Eric didn't think me a criminal made me want to cry. "If Davis is investigating me, then he isn't looking for her."

"That's what I'm thinking too." He leaned back against the table, resting his arms on the top. "She may react violently, no longer just threatening, if her ploy doesn't work."

I straightened. "Do you think that's why Davis is acting like I'm a suspect?"

"Probably." He smiled. "No one in their right

mind would think you a thief and a murderer."

Milton obviously wasn't in his right mind, because the first words out of his mouth upon arriving were, "I knew you weren't the sweet innocent girl you portray yourself as."

I rolled my eyes not giving him the satisfaction of an answer. Instead, I occupied my time confined to the picnic table to figure out how to prove Marcy Wilson or Linda Boyles was the thief. I leaned more toward Marcy. Somehow, I'd find a way to sneak in her house and look around.

Perk sent me a consoling glance and followed Milton into the house as Marcy inched by, watching the law enforcement officers before turning her gaze on me. I shrugged and waved, hoping by doing so she wouldn't guess that I suspected her.

"I need to find a way to get into her house."

"Don't do anything illegal," Eric said. "Davis has threatened to arrest you more than once."

I grinned. "If something breaks in her house, with it being a rental, I'd have to go in to make repairs."

He sighed. "I do not want to hear this."

It didn't take long for the two police officers to step out of my house and head to where Davis stood. A few minutes later, Davis approached us. "The inside is clean."

"Told you I didn't steal anything."

"There is still the matter of the stolen items under your house." His features didn't relax from the stoniness. "We'll be taking them, and we'll be keeping you under surveillance."

"Do what you need to do. I've nothing to hide."

I crossed my arms and glanced past him to where Mags watched us with great interest. The moment the three officers left, she rushed over.

"What's going on? Why is there yellow tape around the bottom of your house?"

"Caper dug up some jewelry. Now, I'm their number-one suspect." Good. Let the Heavenly Acres gossip chain spread the word, starting with my dear old friend who couldn't keep a secret to save her life.

"That's the most ridiculous thing I've ever heard. If the owner of this place finds out, you'll be out of a job."

I hadn't thought of that. I'd have to zip off a quick email and explain it's all a ploy to lay a trap. At least, I hoped that's all it was.

"You've got to put a stop to this, CJ. It's getting out of hand."

"I'm trying, Mags." I told her of Eric's and my early adventure. "We're getting close."

She plopped down across from us. "I would have loved to have gone on a high speed chase with you. I love fast cars."

"Our rental isn't that fast." I glanced at the car, sitting there in broad daylight. If Marcy was the thief, she knew without a doubt it was us who had chased her. "Eric, the car."

"How could we have made a mistake like that?" He palmed his forehead. "I'll go return the car. Don't go anywhere until I get back." He marched away mumbling about bonehead moves.

"What are you planning?" Mags grinned. "I know something is going on in that head of yours."

"I need to throw some breakers. Want to come?" We had a minimum of forty-five minutes before Eric returned, but I only needed ten.

We hurried as fast as Mags could go and I flipped the breakers on house number ten in the large breaker box. Now, when Marcy complained about no electricity, she'd have to let us in. I tacked a note to her door, saying there were issues, and that we'd be entering her home in the morning.

"That gives her enough time to hide things," Mags said. "Do you have to warn her?"

"By law, yes. We might still find something to prove her guilt." We returned to my house and sat exactly where we were when Eric left.

When he returned, he looked at us with suspicion. "I don't believe for a second that you actually stayed here."

"I did get up to go to the bathroom," Mags lied. "Does that count? And CJ got a drink. Otherwise, we've been sitting here trying to come up with another plan. The other ones didn't work well."

He still didn't believe us, but took a seat, placing a bag on the table. "I took the liberty of bringing sub sandwiches. I called Amber, and she'll be joining us."

"I thought we weren't going to talk about the case in the open?" Mags asked.

"At this point, I think we should." Eric handed us each a wrapped Italian sub. "We want the thief to make a move."

I clapped. "Yay. You've fallen to the dark side."

"No, just came to the reluctant conclusion that setting a trap has become a necessity." He glanced up and smiled as Amber joined us.

I squelched down the jealousy. After all, I'd almost received a kiss from him. That had to mean something could be blooming between us. I took a bite of my sandwich. "Thanks for supper."

"Anytime." Eric's eyes twinkled. "We've had quite the day." He explained the chase down the freeway to Amber.

"Wow." She glanced at me. "You seem fine despite all that."

"I was terrified, but then found it thrilling." I grinned.

"But has no desire to repeat the experience," Eric said. "Those are her words verbatim."

"I don't blame her." Amber shuddered. "Now what?"

"CJ is going into Marcy's house in the morning to find out why the electricity isn't working," Mags, said, wiping her mouth with a napkin.

"Mine works fine," Amber said. "Is it only her house?"

I ducked my head. "Maybe." I kicked Mags under the table.

"What did you do?" Eric frowned.

I sighed. "Mags, you have a big mouth. I might have flipped a breaker."

"Might have?" His brows rose. "I knew it was too good to be true to think the two of you had waited at this table for me."

"Now you know not to make ridiculous requests." Mags picked up her sandwich. "You'd think you'd learn by now."

"I'm rather dense when it comes to women and

their devious ways." He tossed me a wink. "I'm willing to learn though."

And…cue the blush.

Amber laughed. "I'm sure you'll get plenty of experience through this escapade."

"Hush." Mags waved her hand in a downward motion. "Number one suspect returning."

We all watched as Marcy drove past, her gaze falling on the yellow tape waving from under my house. First step of the trap a success. Now for step number two. "Mags, I need you to start telling people the police suspect me."

"You'll never fill the rentals that way," she said, shaking her head.

"We'll worry about that when this is all behind us." I rubbed my hands together. It would all fall into place, I felt it in my heart. Lay out the steps, follow the path, and voilà, an arrest.

Mags stood. "I guess I'll start spreading the lie with the Olsons. Tammy has loose lips, bless her heart. Then, I'll move down the line. Not sure how I can bring up the subject in a subtle manner, but I'll think of something."

"I'm sure you will." Her loose-lip comment was a bit like Caper saying she wasn't a dog, but I let it slide. When Mags had shuffled off, I turned to the others. "This will either help or hinder us, but I don't have a better idea."

"It will help." Amber gathered up our trash. "We need to flush this rabbit out of the brush. See you tomorrow. Make sure someone goes with you to check the breaker in number ten."

"I will." I glanced at Eric who nodded.

"Wouldn't dream of letting you go alone." He stood. "I've some patrolling to do, so I'll be here bright and early. What time does Marcy usually leave in the morning?"

"Around seven-thirty."

"Then that's what time I'll be here." His gaze softened and landed on my lips.

This is it. Finally.

"Goodnight, CJ." He smiled and strolled away, leaving me wanting to be kissed so very much.

With a sigh, I snapped my fingers at Caper and went in my house, locking the door against the outside world. I slouched on the sofa, cuddly dog on my lap, and stroked her fur while I went through tomorrow's steps.

Get in, search every single cranny without raising suspicion or getting caught, then bag a murdering thief. Sounded like a huge job, but I felt up to the task. Watch out, Marcy, we're coming to get you.

Chapter Twenty-one

Marcy didn't drive away until almost eight a.m. When she did, Eric and I sprinted for her house. I'd come to the conclusion she didn't hold down a regular nine-to-five job, so we didn't know how much time we had to search.

I had my key in the lock when something hissed behind me. I whirled to see Mags at the foot of the steps. "What?"

"I'm the lookout. I'll make bird calls if Marcy returns while you're in her house."

It couldn't hurt. I glanced at Eric who nodded. A turn of the key and we stepped inside, closing the door behind us. I quickly made note of a window over the sink that we could easily squeeze through if we had to. One always needed a way out. Something else I learned from television shows. I wasn't as bad as Grams had been about believing everything she saw, but there had to be some things of value to take away from a show. Right?

"It barely looks as if someone lives here," Eric

said.

I agreed. A fold-out futon to sleep on, paper plates and plastic utensils, two changes of clothing folded on the counter. I opened the refrigerator. Bottled water, energy drinks, and Chinese leftovers. "She doesn't live here. This is a stopping place." If not here, then where?

"Why the pretense?"

I shrugged. "Let's start looking for…something." Anything, really, to show who this woman was.

"I doubt there's anything of value here, but let's get busy." Eric climbed into the loft. "Lots of boxes up here. One is full of papers."

"Start there." I searched the cabinets, the bathroom, the usual hiding places, and came up empty. No loose floorboards or wall panels. It looked as if the place was nothing more than a storage unit for files.

"I found some old bills, but they're addressed to an Addie Morris," Eric called down.

"Who is she? Anything in those boxes that looks stolen?"

"I haven't gone past this one box. The others are taped shut, so maybe. Hold on. I've got a pocket knife." The sound of cardboard tearing. "We've got three Blu-ray players and what looks like a box that comes from a jeweler. I'd say these could be stolen."

"I agree." I started to close the small pantry when I noticed a phone number written on the inside of the door. I pulled out my cell phone and dialed the number.

"Hello?"

I hung up. Why would Marcy have written down Lenora's phone number on a cabinet door?

"Caw, Caw."

I frowned. Was that supposed to be a bird call?

"Caw, Caw."

"Eric?"

"I hear." He swung down from the loft. "Let's go." Grabbing my hand, we darted outside. I'd barely locked the door and ducked around the corner before Marcy drove up. Once she entered her house, we rushed to the breaker box, turned the electricity back on, and met up with Mags.

"That's the worst bird call I've ever heard." I leaned over, balancing my hands on my knees and fought to catch my breath.

"It's the best I've got."

"I need to let her know I was in the house because of a blown fuse or something."

"Let's make it fast. I need to head to the woods." Eric started for number ten.

"No, it'll look suspicious. I'm the overseer, not you, so I'll visit her in an official capacity."

He didn't look convinced. "It's too dangerous."

"I'm here," Mags said. "I've got my Taser."

"She's not going to do anything in broad daylight with people around. Look." Lucy's children played in the common area with the Olson kids. Lucy sat on her front porch, mug in hand, and supervised. Roy drove by on a golf cart. "See? Busy place on a Saturday."

"All right. Stay together." He cupped my chin. "Stay out of trouble."

"No guarantees." I smiled. I almost told him about Marcy having Lenora's phone number, but held back. He needed to do his job, and by telling him, I'd only delay him. "I'll be careful. I promise."

He gave me a lopsided smile, then jogged for his side-by-side. With a wave, he headed for the trail that went past the campgrounds.

"Stay here," I told Mags. "We're paying Lenora a visit when I'm finished with Marcy."

"Oh, goodie." She sat on a bench near the green area, and I headed back to number ten.

I raised my hand to knock, but the door swung open before I could. "I've come to let you know the electrical problem was nothing more than a blown fuse." I smiled.

"Really?" She tilted her head, a smirk on her face. "You've been inside. You've seen how little I have. How could I have blown a fuse?" She waved a dismissive hand. "Doesn't matter anyway. As you now know, I'm leaving this place."

"But your rent is paid for another month."

She shrugged. "It isn't safe around here. I don't make enough money to risk losing what little I have."

"What do you do anyway?"

"I'm a receptionist. It's on my application. Are we done here? Because I've a few more things to pack up. I hope to be out of here by morning."

I stared at her and she stared right back, both knowing the other was as fake as a glass diamond. I broke the silence first. "No hurry, Marcy. I can't rent this until your lease is up." With a nod, I left and headed back to Mags.

"Guess what I overheard the newlyweds talking about." She motioned her head toward number two. "They were out for a stroll talking about how easy it was to fool someone. Do you think they mean you?"

I frowned. "But Marcy is the thief."

"Are you sure? I mean really sure?" She stood. "You can't rule them out just yet." I told Mags about Marcy having Lenora's phone number, and that Marcy was leaving. "Didn't Lenora say she barely knew her?"

"Yes, but Lenora was the overseer before you. Maybe that's why Marcy had her number."

I shook my head. "We have a phone for work. That's the one tenants are supposed to call. It doesn't add up."

"Then let's go connect some more pieces."

Lenora sighed when she opened the door. "What now?"

"Why does Marcy Wilson have your phone number?" I crossed my arms. "There's no need to invite us in; just answer some questions."

"I don't have to tell you anything." She tried to close the door.

I stopped it with my foot. "Something is rotten in Heavenly Acres, and you know more than you're letting on."

"You're a fool, CJ Turley, and your nose is going to get you in a heap of trouble. You can't go around accusing people of crimes." She shoved the door against my foot.

I kept an impassive face despite the pain and kept my foot firmly in place. "Do you know Marcy or not?"

"Of course, I do. She's a regular in the tiny house community."

"Do you know Addie Morris?"

Her eyes widened. "Where did you hear that name?"

"Do you?"

"No." She pressed harder on the door. "Move your foot or have it cut off. Get off my property before I call the cops."

"Go ahead and call."

She grinned. "Last I heard, you were a prime suspect in the thefts."

"Where did you hear that?"

"A little birdie." She gave me a shove, then slammed the door as I stumbled back.

"That was an unpleasant exchange," Mags said.

"I'm the one whose foot was crushed." I sat on the step, removed my shoe, and rubbed where the door had creased my arch. "All you did was stand there and let me do all the talking. Why so silent all of a sudden?"

"I was busy taking it all in. Want to know what I noticed while you played battle of the wits?" Her eyes sparkled. "The garage door was open a bit, and it's piled with boxes. I bet Lenora is also planning on skedaddling. I'm also willing to predict that she and Marcy are in cahoots with each other. You need to find out how those two are connected."

"First, I want to tell Davis about Addie Morris so they can look into her."

"Let's look first, but not here. Lenora is peeking through the curtains."

I glared over my shoulders before hobbling to the car. Once I was in the driver's seat, I typed Addie Morris into the search engine and found myself staring at the social media profile of a woman who looked exactly like Marcy Wilson.

I drove to the police station as fast as I could without breaking any laws. Milton was exiting the building as Mags and I entered.

He smirked. "Ready to turn yourself in?"

"You wish." Oh, I wanted to tell him what we'd discovered so badly, but since I couldn't stand the man, I did nothing more than return his smirk and approach the reception desk.

"We'd like to see Detective Davis, please."

"He's not in," the woman said. "Will Officer Perk suffice?"

"Sure."

She spoke into her headset, then turned her attention back to us. "He said to go back."

"Thank you." We took a seat in the bull pen across from Perk. "Marcy Wilson is really Addie Morris. There has to be a significant reason for her to use an alias, don't you think?"

The quiet officer nodded. "Does seem shady."

"Will you pass the information to Davis to check out?"

"Yes, ma'am. I'll give it to him the minute he comes back." His smile seemed forced in his dark face.

I chalked it up to stress from not being able to catch the thief. "I hope this info helps you solve this. Summer tourist season is coming."

"I understand." He stood. "Let me walk you out.

You ladies be careful, you hear? Davis doesn't like you snooping." He escorted us through the reception area and back outside.

As Mags and I returned to my car, I glanced back to see a stern-faced Perk still watching. I gave a wave he didn't return, then slid into the driver's seat. "Does he seem off to you?"

"Not really," Mags said. "He's always been quiet. Milton's the one who rubs me wrong."

"Hmm." I drove home and filled out the monthly report to send to the owner, also letting them know about the ruse with me as the prime suspect. It wouldn't be good for him to find out through the grapevine. I hit send, poured a big glass of ice tea, and took it outside.

From my chair on the porch, I watched the sun set over the lake. Eric usually stopped by after a day's work. Maybe he'd got hung up and would stop by tomorrow. I wanted to fill him in on the latest development.

Instead, I was content to watch as my tiny community settled in for the night. I got up and moved to the narrow gravel road. A light still burned in number ten, letting me know Marcy hadn't left yet. I hoped she stuck around long enough for Davis to question her. Once she left, she wouldn't be easily found.

Lucy yelled for her brood to come and eat. The television flickered from the newlyweds' tent. Mags' cat lounged on her windowsill. Amber's dark house meant she was working a late shift. I peered through the dimming light of dusk at movement near number ten.

I returned to the porch, set my glass on the table, and headed toward number ten, keeping to the darkening shadows. I couldn't make out his features, but a man did the same thing, staying in the dark. When he reached Marcy's house, he darted inside without knocking.

Should I shout out a warning? Maybe the woman had a boyfriend I didn't know about. If so, why all the secrecy…unless—

I glanced to where Dave Lincoln lived. No lights on at his place. Could the widower be wooing two female residents at the same time? If so, he'd be the envy of any man who found out. Lucy was spotted most nights at his place. If he also spent time with Marcy, when did he sleep? I chuckled. None of my business, but did he know he was wooing a thief and a murderer?

"Boo."

I clapped a hand over my mouth and whirled. "Not funny, Eric."

"Why are you skulking around out here by yourself?"

"I spotted a man going into Marcy's house." I quickly filled him in on the day's events. "If Marcy is seeing Dave Lincoln, which is just speculation at this point, was she the woman who killed Ronnie Ward? If so, why? And why hide stolen goods so close to where they were taken in the first place? This web is getting more and more tangled."

Chapter Twenty-two

When I didn't hear from Davis by the middle of the next day after giving Perk the message, I phoned him myself. Something I should have done instead of going to the police station, but I thought a face-to-face would make him listen to me.

"Detective Davis."

"DJ. Turley. Did Officer Perk give you my message yesterday?"

"No. What was it?"

"That Marcy Wilson may actually be Addie Morris." I explained how I'd discovered her alias. "Yesterday, I had to go into her house to check out some faulty wiring, and Eric found a box full of electronics. I found a phone number in a cabinet. The number belongs to Lenora Rice, the very woman who said she didn't know Marcy very well." I spewed out all that I'd learned, then waited for the explosion.

"Let me get this straight. You entered the suspect's home on a ruse, riffled through her belongings, then went to speak with a possible accomplice. Did I get it right?"

"Pretty much," I mumbled. "But look at the bright side. We uncovered some valuable information."

His sigh practically vibrated the air waves. "I'm on my way. Do. Not. Go anywhere." Click.

Well, that went as expected. I grinned and propped my feet on the railing of my tiny porch, coffee in hand, and waited for an irate detective to arrive. Hopefully, Eric would get here first to act as a buffer.

Mags wandered by carrying a big stick. "Good morning."

"Same to you. What's the stick for?"

"Since we're getting close to cornering this killer, I thought it best to have another weapon. In addition to my Taser, of course. I spent some time this morning in the chapel. A wonderful way to begin a Sunday morning." She plopped down on the bottom step. "Who are we waiting for?"

"Detective Davis."

"Are you in trouble again?"

"Most likely."

We laughed, then Mags said, "I'm glad you moved here, girl. You liven up the place."

"Davis wouldn't agree." I put my feet down as the detective arrived. "He thinks I'm a problem."

"From the angry look on his handsome face, I agree."

"Ladies." He glanced from Mags to me. "Since Ms. Snyder is here, I assume she's a part of all this?"

"If you mean did she go with me to talk to Lenora, then yes." I grinned.

"I'm her sidekick," Mags said. "Every great sleuth has one."

"CJ is not a sleuth. Neither are you. All the two of you do is make my job more difficult."

"How so?" My smile faded and I crossed my arms. "I've given you new information every time we've had a conversation. That's more than Milton or Perk have done. Or you, for that matter."

His eyes flashed. "Where is Eric?"

"Hasn't shown up this morning." Which kind of concerned me, truth be told. "He does have another job other than babysitting me."

"Since you obviously have a key to Ms. Wilson's house, I need you to come with me and let me in." Clearly, it pained him to ask anything of me.

"I'm happy to be of assistance." I set my mug on the railing and led the way to number ten.

The house looked abandoned in the way you can usually tell without stepping a foot inside. Marcy must have left sometime in the night with her mystery man, unless the man was Dave Lincoln, who watched us with interest from his porch. I'd speak to him when we were finished here.

I unlocked the door. Sure enough, it sat as empty as the day Marcy moved in. All evidence of her stealing was gone. She'd gotten away again.

Davis strode past me and stopped in the middle of the living space. "It doesn't appear as if anything is left, but I'll look."

"Don't you usually have Milton or Perk do

that?"

"Milton is busy, and Perk took a vacation."

"In the middle of a murder investigation?" I didn't believe it. I'd spoken to the officer yesterday. Now, with him being gone and not having given Davis my message, suspicion grew inside me like a vine. "You don't know where he is, do you? Is it possible he was the man here with Marcy last night?"

Davis spun to face me. "Why do you say that?"

"I'm suspicious of just about everyone right now. Last night's man stuck to the shadows, but he clearly slipped into her house. Now Perk is gone, as is Marcy. And he never gave you my message."

"My gut instinct tells me I might be onto something. Think about it." I searched his face, silently imploring him to consider my idea. "If Perk knows Marcy is the guilty party, then he wouldn't have mentioned I came by the station. He would have warned her that I knew who she was."

He took me by the arm and escorted me from the house. I could tell Davis was considering what I said, although he would never admit it. "Contact Eric and have him come get you. You can patrol with him."

Nodding, I unclipped the radio from my belt. Eric's radio was off. "That's strange."

"Go home with Mags, CJ, and stay there."

"I have a dog. Mags has a cat. They don't like each other."

"Then go home." He hurried to his car and sped away.

His behavior ignited a flicker of fear in me.

Where was Eric?

Mags stared after the car. "I guess we should go home and lock our doors. I hate hiding, though. These tiny houses could be traps with no back doors."

"I need to talk to Dave Lincoln first." Then I might go home, but I doubted it. If Eric was in trouble, I needed to find him. Hiding would accomplish nothing. Well, maybe it would keep me from being killed, but Eric was more important.

Mags and I hurried to Dave's porch. I had no time to waste on trivial conversation and got right to the point. "Did you visit Marcy last night?"

His brow furrowed. "Why would I do that?"

"Are you seeing her?"

"I'm seeing Lucy." He laughed. "I'm too old to juggle two women. The only man I've seen sneaking in and out of her house is that young cop."

I glanced at Mags. "Bingo." On the way to my house, I dialed Davis. "I have a witness who's seen Perk visiting Marcy at a late hour."

"Go home. Seriously, CJ." Click.

I called him back. "Not until I find out if Eric is in trouble. You'll have to arrest me to keep me tied down." This time I hung up on him. "In the cart, Mags. We're on the hunt."

"Where? These woods are a big place."

"Just hold on. I'm following the regular trails. If I don't see anything, we'll venture off."

"We need water and snacks. Can't rush away unprepared." We stopped at her place for the needed items, then picked up Caper before heading down the trail.

Clouds gathered overhead, promising rain. I hoped the downpour would wait until we found Eric and returned home. A low rumble of thunder sounded. I secured Caper with a belt between Mags and me, then increased our speed.

"When I said I liked high-speed chases," Mags said, holding on to the dashboard, "I didn't mean in a golf cart. Slow down or you'll turn us over."

"No, I won't." I slid to a halt next to the chapel. With the darkening sky, the cross should have been lit. Some party pooper had turned it off. I'd deal with that later. Not finding any sign of Eric there, I kept going.

"We need Amber. She can track."

I agreed. "But she's at work. I'm doing the best I can." With no rain in over a week, the trail was dry with no new tire tracks.

Turning left, we sped through the campground, stopping in front of Mr. Robinson's. "Have you seen Eric?"

"He stopped by this morning. Said he was following someone."

"Did he say where?"

"Through the woods." He peered closer at me. "Is everything alright?"

"He isn't answering his radio."

"He's most likely out of range. Don't worry. Ranger can take care of himself. But if you're intent on going after him, he headed west." He pointed behind us.

"Thanks." I circled and rocketed off.

"Who was that fine-looking man?" Mags raised her eyebrows. "I like them tall and thin, brooding, with all their hair. Maybe I need to rent a campsite."

"Mr. Robinson. He runs the campground. Confirmed bachelor." I grinned. "Maybe you can change his mind."

"Maybe I can." She shrieked and held on again as I swerved left down a path clearly used for four-wheeled vehicles of the recreational type.

Grass grew up between the tire tracks. Ruts made our ride bouncy, almost tossing Mags from her seat a time or two. The sky darkened as the clouds overhead thickened. We were going to get soaked. I doubted the canvas covering on the cart would protect us much.

I slowed and tried the radio again. Still nothing. It had a five-mile radius, which meant it had been turned off. A shiver of dread spiraled down my spine. He wouldn't turn it off unless forced to.

"You're getting worried." Mags placed a hand on my arm.

"Yes, I am. I haven't known Eric long, but it doesn't seem like him."

"Maybe he turned off his radio so it wouldn't give away his position when someone called him."

"Maybe." Oh, God, I hoped that was the reason. What if my snooping had made him the next victim? I'd never forgive myself.

The path curved again, providing a glimpse of the lake between the trees. A ranger station rose overhead. I'd not noticed it before, but then I'd never been this deep in the forest. I sure hoped I could find our way out.

Mags unwrapped a protein bar and opened a bottle of water, setting both on the seat between my legs. "Got to keep your strength up since we're lost."

"How'd you guess?"

"I've noticed that tree split by lightening twice now." She opened another bottle and took a drink. "Keep the lake on the right. We'll get out eventually. These four-wheeler paths always lead out."

"That's good to know." I drove slower, glancing to my left, then to my right. "Look." I hit the brakes, sending a cloud of dust into the air. "Eric's side-by-side."

Pulled off the trail behind a thick brush was Eric's vehicle. I turned off the golf cart and dashed to the vehicle. No sign of foul play. It was as if he'd parked and taken a stroll. I wanted to call out for him but didn't want to give him away if he had Marcy in his sights.

I started back to the golf cart as lightning struck the tree in front of me.

Chapter Twenty-three

The tree fell toward the golf cart as if in slow motion. Mags rolled to the ground, taking Caper with her. The clouds opened, releasing their burden of rain in a torrent. "Mags!"

A branch clipped my shoulder, knocking me to the already sodden ground and pinned me like a bug to a board in mud, which was turning to liquid under the deluge of rain. "Caper," I called, blinking against the drops assaulting my face.

My dog pushed through the leaves and licked my face. "Good girl. Where's Mags?"

Caper whined and sat next to me. This couldn't be good. Mags would be here too, if she were able. I squirmed, trying to free myself. "I can't feel my left arm, girl. Wish you were like Lassie and could go for help."

As the rain poured and time passed, I sank deeper into the mud, becoming more and more worried about not only Mags' welfare, but my own. I didn't want to drown in the woods pinned under a tree. My left arm remained useless, and my right side burned. I tried again to push against the thick branch with my good arm. Sometimes, being petite was a curse.

"Hey." Mags appeared above me, leaning on the branch. Blood dripped down her face. "You okay?"

"Don't lean on the branch, please." I groaned.

"Sorry." She straightened. "Don't think I can move this off you."

"Is the cart drivable?"

"I think so. The top is dented in, but I can slouch."

"You need to find help. I'm sinking fast." Fear tinged my words with trembling.

"I'll get something to lift your head out of the mud." She gently lodged a smaller branch under my head. Not comfortable, but effective for now. "I don't know how long I'll be gone." Worry creased her face. "Stay alive, okay?"

"I'll do my best." I pulled Caper on top of me, gaining warmth and comfort from her little body. "Stay to the right."

She smiled. "I've heard that somewhere before." Then she was gone.

Helpless tears mixed with the rain. My cell phone would be useless in my drenched pocket. My fingers strained to reach the radio on my belt, hoping, praying that Eric would answer. A shout of relief came out as my hand finally closed around the device. I pressed the talk button. "Eric?" Nothing but silence. "Please...I need your help. I'm pinned under a tree and I'm going to drown. Please, hear me." A sob choked off my words. "Eric?" My arm fell into the mud as my sobs increased.

Pain riddled my body, I sank deeper into the mire. Caper whimpered and shivered. No one could hear my cries. Who knew I'd died at the hand of mother nature instead of Marcy? I'd imagined a showdown between her and me. Since I'd never killed anyone, she'd win, but not before I let Davis know where we were. Justice would be served. Now…it was up to Davis and Milton, and only one of them had a brain.

Maybe if I concentrated on the case, I could forget my pain and the shivering cold. Point number one: Marcy and Perk were both gone. Conclusion, they were together. While it was possible Perk was working undercover to catch her, I wasn't sold on the idea. Point number two: I was freezing. My brain refused to work, but thank the Lord above, the rain had slowed.

I tried the radio again. "Eric, please."

The radio crackled. My heart leaped. "CJ?"

I started to cry again.

"Baby, where are you?"

"Under a tree," I wailed.

"Where?"

"I don't know. Mags went to get help. We got lost looking for you."

"Why were you looking for me?"

"I got worried. You always come see me before and after work."

He chuckled. "You sweet thing." He grew silent as my cries increased, then asked, "Are you alright?"

"I'm pinned under a tree in the mud, and I can't

feel my left arm." The radio beeped, signaling a low battery. "Oh, no."

"Which path did you follow?" He panted as if running.

"We saw your side-by-side. We're further than that."

"I'll be—" The radio died.

I took a deep shuddering breath. Eric would come for me. I hugged Caper tighter against me. "Almost saved, little girl."

She whimpered and rested her head on my arm.

I closed my eyes and let sleep overtake me. Shouting woke me up. The rain had stopped. Someone called my name. "I'm here," I managed.

More than one set of feet thudded toward me. "Help me get this off her, Amber," Eric ordered.

"I couldn't find Eric," Mags said, "so I fetched Amber. Then we caught up with Eric on the way."

"Thank you." I gritted my teeth against the pain of them lifting the branch. Once I was free, Amber knelt beside me.

"I think her arm is broken and the branch scraped up her side pretty good." She dug in a canvas bag she'd brought. "I have an inflated splint that will suffice until we get you to the hospital." She uncorked a bottle of water and held out a white pill. "For the pain. Open up."

I obeyed and let her place the tablet on my tongue, then took a sip of the water. "Just get me out of here, please."

Once Amber had the splint on my arm, Eric scooped me up and sprinted for the side-by-side. Every bounce sent pain ricocheting through me, but

I didn't care. I snuggled against his strong chest and let him save me until I gave into darkness again.

I woke in a hospital bed with Eric sitting in a green vinyl chair next to me. He smiled as he caught me gazing at him. I'd never seen a more wonderful sight than that man with mussed hair and a mud-smeared ranger uniform. "Why'd you turn off your radio?"

Taking my hand in his, he rubbed his thumb back and forth across my skin. "I followed Marcy and Perk last night as far as I could. I didn't want the radio to alert Perk to my presence. I'm so sorry." He raised my good hand to his lips.

"I thought something horrible had happened to you."

"The fact you cared so much to come after me fills my heart with more joy than I can express." His gaze warmed. "Clarice Josephine, don't ever do that again, though. I couldn't bear anything happening to you."

I smiled. "No guarantees."

A man in a white coat entered the room and lifted the clipboard containing my chart from a holder on the wall. "It's good to see you awake, Miss Turley. How are you feeling?"

"Pretty good, actually." I raised the bed to a sitting position. "I'm ready to go home."

"Tomorrow. We'd like to keep you tonight. You had quite a day." He glanced up and smiled. "Hypothermia, broken arm, scraped side, loss of consciousness...need I go on?"

"I guess not." I sighed.

"From what the two ladies waiting to see you

said, I gather you're a hard woman to keep down. This is one way to make sure you get at least one good night's rest. I'll see you in the morning."

As soon as he left, Amber and Mags took his place. A white bandage peeked from under Mags' silver-streaked hair. "It's good to see you awake," she said. "You scared us."

"I was worried about you. When that tree fell, you didn't answer my calls."

She tapped her bandage. "Hit my head. I reckon I got knocked out, but don't tell the doctor. I told him I was conscious the whole time. I'm not spending the night in this germ trap."

"You're here now, Grandma." Amber put an arm around her shoulder. "Plus, I work here and take offense at that remark."

Mags shrugged. "I call things as I see them."

I loved these people. "Thank you for brightening my day. I get out in the morning." My eyes drooped.

"That's our cue, folks," Eric said. "Time to go." He glanced at me. "I'll be here to take you home."

"I'm working tonight," Amber said, "so I'll keep a good eye on you."

"Looks like you're my ride home, handsome." Mags winked at Eric, who laughed.

He crooked his arm. "My pleasure."

My eyes were fully closed before they left the room.

When I awoke, the room's light had been lowered to dim. Curtains on the window blocked out the moonlight, but someone was sitting in a chair across the room. My nerves tingled. "Who's there?"

The figure unfolded and drew close enough for me to make out Perk's features. "Oh, I was right. You are working undercover." I'd say anything to keep him from killing me. Of course, if that was his intention, I'd be dead already, right?

"Is that what you believe?" His eyes widened.

"Of course. You're a police officer. It's part of the job, isn't it?" My heart skipped a beat and not in the good way it did when Eric paid me a compliment. I shot a glance toward the door. Not closed, but only open a few inches. My hand inched toward the nurse call button.

"I wouldn't if I were you." He gripped a pillow in his hands.

"You're here to kill me? Why didn't you while I was sleeping?"

"Since I'd managed to sneak into your room, I decided to take a little nap. I'm not one for running through a forest." He stepped closer.

"Why?"

"Why kill you? Because you're a nuisance. Addie and I had a good thing going until you arrived on the scene, sticking your nose where it didn't belong. Tiny house residents and the campers provided us with plenty of trinkets to steal and sell."

"Where is Addie?" I now knew without a doubt that Marcy and Addie were the same person.

" I'll not divulge that information, Miss Turley." He grinned without humor and loomed over me.

I opened my mouth to scream as he pressed the pillow over my face. I pounded his side with my good hand, but could only reach as far as the IV would allow. I kicked and thrashed, trying to free my face. Black spots danced in front of my eyes.

A shot rang out and the pressure released.

I pulled the pillow from my face.

Davis stood in the doorway, gun still aimed to where Perk had fallen. He cut me a glance. "Still breathing?"

"Barely." I sucked air into my lungs. "Thanks. How did you know?"

"Amber called me. She recognized Perk as he entered the building." He knelt over the body. "He's dead."

"He wouldn't tell me where Addie was." I pushed to a sitting position. "I really wanted to know. Almost dying twice in one day is getting old."

Davis shot me an amused glance. "You're something else." He straightened. "Don't worry about Addie Morris. She'll turn up."

"That's what I'm afraid of." I fell back to sleep.

Chapter Twenty-four

The next morning, Eric took me home to a welcoming committee. Amber, Davis, Milton, and Mags sat around my picnic table. I had to admit to being surprised to see Milton.

As if he could read my mind, the officer said, "I'm here to be your bodyguard." He sounded as pleased about the prospect as I was. Which wasn't much. Milton yanked the yellow crime-scene tape from around my house and tossed it in a nearby garbage can.

I glanced at the doughnuts and coffee. "Wow, I should get injured more often."

"No," Eric said, pulling up a folding chair. "I'd prefer you didn't."

"Tell us what Perk told you before I shot him," Davis said, his face grave.

"First, he took a nap. Then he said he had to kill me because I was nosy," I held up my hand to stop the remarks that were sure to come. "And that he and Addie had a good thing before I came along. He

195

wouldn't tell me where she is. That's it."

"Which means she'll now seek retaliation because her man is dead and CJ isn't," Mags said. "That's what I would do in her situation."

"You aren't helping," Amber added. "There's no need for CJ to be more frightened than she already is."

"I'm not scared." I glanced from one face to the next. "I'm surrounded by friends who care about me. I beat death twice yesterday. If the grim reaper does show up in the form of Addie Morris, I've had a blast." She would come, and I'd be ready, but I hoped she'd give me time to recover from yesterday.

"Are you tired? Do you want to go to bed?" Eric studied me.

"No, I'm fine. I can take a nap later." I glanced at Davis. "I didn't thank you for saving me last night."

"Part of the job. I hate that one of my men turned out to be a bad cop."

"I always thought something was off about him," Milton said.

"Sure, you did." Davis smirked, muttering something about ineptness. I wasn't sure if he meant Milton, himself, or both. Either way, you'd think one of them would have caught on.

"I have to take Davis to try and pick up Addie's trail," Eric said. "With Milton here, you should be safe. I'll see you at supper. Chinese?"

"Sounds wonderful." I grinned.

"That leaves us with nothing to do," Mags said after the two men left. "It's back to the normal life of housework and gardening. How boring."

"Speak for yourself," Amber said. "Summer means more injuries and more work hours for me."

My work would also increase as the rest of the rentals filled with vacationers coming and going. I looked forward to something to fill my day after Addie was put behind bars.

Roy stopped his cart in front of us. "CJ, do you have a minute?"

"Sure." I moved to his side. "I may have a broken arm, but I'm still working."

He lowered his voice. "I found a gas can near the chapel. Looks like someone's planning on burning it to the ground."

"Did you dispose of it?"

"I thought you might want to take a look."

"I would. I'll get Milton and meet you there in five minutes." I hurried back to the others. "Officer Milton, there's something I need to investigate. Since I only have one working arm, I need you to drive." I dug the cart keys from my pocket and tossed them to him.

He caught them with his right hand. "Good. Something to do rather than sit here all day."

My sentiments exactly. I climbed into the passenger seat and held on with my good hand as Milton raced after Roy. All that was missing was a siren and blinking red and blue lights. Now I knew how Mags felt when I rocketed across the grounds.

When we reached the path leading to the chapel, Milton hit the brakes. With the ground still wet from yesterday's downpour, the cart slid into the back of Roy's. He spun around and glared. "Drive much, Officer?"

"Cars, not carts." Milton turned off the ignition and climbed out. "Lead the way, Mr. Olson."

Roy rolled his eyes and headed down the path to the back of the chapel. "Right here." He pointed to a red plastic gas can. "I might have surprised them this morning."

"Why burn down the chapel?" Milton asked.

"My guess," I said with a shudder, "is Addie wants to lure everyone away from me, thus giving her access to finish what Perk failed to do."

"That's quite a leap, Miss Turley," Milton said, shaking his head. "She would have no way of making sure we all left your side."

"If there was a fire, wouldn't you go investigate?" I tilted my head.

"Most likely."

"With Eric and Davis gone, the only armed person in the group would have left me."

A light brightened in his eyes. "I see your point." Using a handkerchief, he lifted the gas can and placed it in the back of the cart. "No matter what happens, I will not leave your side."

I might survive Addie's wrath after all. We drove back to my house, where I climbed to the loft to take a nap with Caper, leaving Milton downstairs to flip through channels on the television.

Once in bed, I lay on my back, my arm throbbing, and stared at the ceiling. Amber would insist I take a pain pill, but my gut told me I needed to stay as alert as possible. A storm was coming, and I needed to weather through without putting any of the people I cared about in danger.

From the television downstairs, I heard a news report about Perk's death and the ongoing hunt for Addie Morris. I doubted anyone would call the station with her whereabouts, but it wouldn't hurt to put out an alert. "Lenora."

"Did you say something?" Milton called up.

"Lenora Rice. She knows Addie. I bet she can give us an idea where she's hiding."

"Unfortunately, we don't have the manpower to send someone to her residence."

"You'll have to go. I'll lock myself in the house and wait for your return."

He shook his head. "I'll lose my job for sure."

"Not if you're responsible for catching a killer." I peered from the top floor. "Think about it. Officer Milton, the hero, the man responsible for bringing a murderer to justice."

"I do like that idea." He stared up at me. "You going to stay in bed like a good girl?"

I crossed my heart. "Most definitely. I've had enough adventure, thank you, and I am very tired." That was the truth. The pain from my arm and side filled me with exhaustion, and nothing sounded better than to sleep the afternoon and night away. "The code to my front door is 1234."

"Change that stupid code immediately." He hooked his gun belt around his paunch. "Stay inside."

"Yes, sir." I smiled and climbed back in bed. Yep, things were coming to a boil. Between Milton questioning Lenora, and Eric and Davis combing the woods, Addie would be caught by morning. I felt it in my bones.

I awoke to darkness. "Milton?" The man should have been back. I climbed from bed and carefully navigated the steps to the bottom floor. Parting the curtains, I peered outside. No sign of him or his squad car. Perhaps he'd gotten a lead to pursue.

Letting the curtain fall back into place, I flipped on the light over the kitchen counter before opening the fridge to find something to eat. Where was the Chinese food Eric had promised? How strange that no one was around.

I pressed the button on the radio. "Eric?"

"You're back?"

"Where did I go?"

"I got a text saying Milton took you to the store."

"Milton went to talk to Lenora while I slept. He's been gone for hours. Something happened."

"Where are you?"

"I'm at home with the doors locked."

"Stay there. Davis and I are on our way."

Not a problem. I grabbed the last slice of leftover pizza from the fridge. A few soft beeps and my front door opened.

"You're not too bright, CJ Turley." Addie smirked. "Using 1234 for your code? Really? Let's go, so I don't have to shoot the handsome ranger or good-looking detective." She aimed a gun at my face.

"What did you do to Milton?"

"Nothing. My mother handled him."

I leaped to my feet. "Lenora is your mother?"

"Surprise." She jabbed me with the gun. "Let's go to the chapel. You can pray before I kill you. Get in the cart and make it snappy. I need this over with before your help arrives."

Since she didn't seem inclined to shoot me there, I took my time leaving the house and climbing into the cart. Once she was in, I rocketed down the drive, hoping she'd fall out. No such luck. She gripped the dash with one hand and aimed the gun at me with the other.

"Nice try." She grinned. "I'm going to enjoy the next few minutes with you."

At least one of us was having fun. I stopped the cart where it seemed to be a lot. Addie prodded me in the back toward the chapel. I couldn't go there. If I did, I was dead.

"Why the chapel?"

"You were the one responsible for rebuilding it and filling this community with hope."

"O-kay. That makes absolutely no sense."

"It doesn't have to. As for killing you, you were responsible for the death of the man I loved, the end of a nice income, and an all-around pain in my rear." She jabbed me harder. "Pick up the pace."

"Why Ronnie?"

"Because the man was loaded and should have given me an enormous engagement ring. One I could accidentally lose, shed a few fake tears at it going missing, then sell for a good profit. When I realized he had no intentions of ever marrying me, not that I would have gone through with a ceremony, well...let's just say he asked too many questions and figured out what I was up to."

"You're an evil woman." I whirled, bashed her in the head with my cast, and screamed as pain ripped up my arm. She stumbled, dropping the gun. Not wasting anymore time, I cradled my broken arm against my side and dashed into the brush toward the cross. The large cross was my only chance at getting away. It could be seen for quite a distance.

I strained to see through the dark. No moon left the woods black as a cauldron. If Addie raced ahead of me, I'd probably plow right into her... or a bear. I opted for the bear. Less greedy, less out for vengeance.

The gleam of the cross drew me to my left. I hunkered down behind it, felt for the on switch, and waited.

The snap of a twig caused my muscles to tense. One, two, three, I threw the switch, illuminating the woods with the glory of a nine-foot cross.

Marcy, err Addie, cursed.

Not blinded, having been on the back side of the cross, I darted out and hit her with my good shoulder, knocking her to the ground. I stepped on her wrist and wrestled the gun from her hand while she shielded her eyes with her left hand. Then I stepped back and trained the gun on her.

"How's that?" It was my turn to grin.

"I hate you."

"Ditto." I motioned the gun toward the path. "Back to the cart."

She wavered between cursing and offering to pay me off to let her go. I let her ramble, wanting nothing more than a pain pill and my bed. Hitting her upside the head with my cast had been a smart move, but a painful one.

"CJ." Eric's voice sounded close.

"We're here." We stepped from the path and into his sight.

He left the cart and rushed toward us, taking possession of the weapon. "Good job, CJ. No one would guess who had an aversion to guns."

"Still hate them, but this time it was necessary." I sagged against the cart. "Where's Davis?"

"On his way. He went to check on Milton. Seems Lenora hit him over the head with a crystal vase. Knocked him out cold." He handcuffed Addie. "Highway patrol stopped Lenora a few miles from town. These two ladies will be locked up for a good long while." He helped Addie into the side-by-side. "Meet you at your house." He gave me a questioning look.

"Right behind you." No rocketing down the pathway, we headed home at a much slower pace, kinder to my aching body. Davis waited for us next to his squad car and took over custody of Addie.

"Good job, CJ." He gave me a nod, then climbed into the car and left.

"I'm so glad that's over. I could sleep for a week."

Eric cupped my face in his hands. "Too tired for that kiss that was stolen from us?"

My gaze locked with his. My lips parted.

He lowered his head, placing his lips on mine and made me forget all about my broken arm as my good arm circled his neck. I returned his kiss with all the passion that had been bottled up inside me for years. My first real kiss would go down in the history books and well worth the wait.

When neither of us could breathe easily, Eric leaned his forehead against mine. "Wow. See you in the morning?"

"Yes." I smiled, touched my finger to his lips, then entered my tiny house. I closed the door and leaned against the wood. "I'll definitely see you tomorrow."

The End

Dear Reader,

It's always a lot fun to begin a new series, and No Small Caper was no exception. I hope you've fallen in love with this cast of characters as much as I have. If you enjoyed this book, please leave a review. They mean a lot to an author.

God Bless,
Cynthia Hickey

Website at www.cynthiahickey.com

Multi-published and Amazon and ECPA Best-Selling author Cynthia Hickey has sold close to a million copies of her works since 2013. She has taught a Continuing Education class at the 2015 American Christian Fiction Writers conference, several small ACFW chapters and RWA chapters, and small writer retreats. She and her husband run the small press, Winged Publications, which includes some of the CBA's best well-known authors. She lives in Arizona and Arkansas, becoming a snowbird, with her husband and one dog. She has nine grandchildren who keep her busy and tell everyone they know that "Nana is a writer".

> Connect with me on FaceBook
> Twitter
> Bookbub
> Sign up for my newsletter and receive a free short story
> www.cynthiahickey.com

> Follow me on Amazon

Enjoy other books by Cynthia Hickey

Fantasy (written as Cynthia Melton)
Fate of the Faes
Shayna
Deema
Kasdeya

Time Travel
The Portal

A Hollywood Murder
Killer Pose, book 1
Killer Snapshot, book 2
Shoot to Kill, book 3
Kodak Kill Shot, book 4
To Snap a Killer

Shady Acres Mysteries
Beware the Orchids, book 1
Path to Nowhere
Poison Foliage
Poinsettia Madness
Deadly Greenhouse Gases
Vine Entrapment

CLEAN BUT GRITTY

Highland Springs

Murder Live
Say Bye to Mommy
To Breathe Again

Colors of Evil Series

Shades of Crimson
Coral Shadows

The Pretty Must Die Series

Ripped in Red, book 1
Pierced in Pink, book 2
Wounded in White, book 3
Worthy, The Complete Story

Lisa Paxton Mystery Series

Eenie Meenie Miny Mo
Jack Be Nimble
Hickory Dickory Dock

One Hour (A short story thriller)

INSPIRATIONAL
(scroll down to see clean books without inspirational
message)

Whisper Sweet Nothings (a short romance)

Nosy Neighbor Series
Anything For A Mystery, Book 1
A Killer Plot, Book 2
Skin Care Can Be Murder, Book 3
Death By Baking, Book 4
Jogging Is Bad For Your Health, Book 5
Poison Bubbles, Book 6
A Good Party Can Kill You, Book 7 (Final)
Nosy Neighbor collection

Christmas with Stormi Nelson

The Summer Meadows Series
Fudge-Laced Felonies, Book 1
Candy-Coated Secrets, Book 2
Chocolate-Covered Crime, Book 3
Maui Macadamia Madness, Book 4
All four novels in one collection

The River Valley Mystery Series
Deadly Neighbors, Book 1
Advance Notice, Book 2

The Librarian's Last Chapter, Book 3
All three novels in one collection

Historical cozy
Hazel's Quest

Historical Romances
Runaway Sue
Taming the Sheriff
Sweet Apple Blossom
A Doctor's Agreement
A Lady Maid's Honor
A Touch of Sugar
Love Over Par
Heart of the Emerald

Finding Love the Harvey Girl Way
Cooking With Love
Guiding With Love
Serving With Love
Warring With Love
All 4 in 1

A Wild Horse Pass Novel
They Call Her Mrs. Sheriff, book 1 (A Western
Romance)

Finding Love in Disaster
The Rancher's Dilemma
The Teacher's Rescue
The Soldier's Redemption

Woman of courage Series

A Love For Delicious
Ruth's Redemption
Charity's Gold Rush
Mountain Redemption
Woman of Courage series (all four books)

Short Story Westerns
Desert Rose
Desert Lilly
Desert Belle
Desert Daisy
Flowers of the Desert 4 in 1

Romantic Suspense

Overcoming Evil series
Mistaken Assassin
Captured Innocence
Mountain of Fear
Exposure at Sea
A Secret to Die for
Collision Course
Romantic Suspense of 5 books in 1

The Game
Suspicious Minds
After the Storm
Local Betrayal

Contemporary

Romance in Paradise
Maui Magic
Sunset Kisses
Deep Sea Love
3 in 1

Finding a Way Home
Service of Love
Hillbilly Cinderella
Unraveling Love
I'd Rather Kiss My Horse

Christmas

Romancing the Fabulous Cooper Brothers
Handcarved Christmas
The Payback Bride
Curtain Calls and Christmas Wishes
Christmas Gold
A Christmas Stamp
Snowflake Kisses
A Christmas Deception

The Red Hat's Club (Contemporary novellas)

Finally
Suddenly
Surprisingly
The Red Hat's Club 3 – in 1

Short Story

One Hour (A short story thriller)
Whisper Sweet Nothings (a Valentine short romance)

49764618R00131

Made in the USA
Lexington, KY
23 August 2019